The Wife in the Wardrobe
(A collection of darkish humorous stories)

By

S. M. Walker

This book is dedicated to my wonderful Italian son,
Matteo.
When he was a little boy, he thought I was calling
him my Sun.
You are my Sun. Thank you for being you.

"It struck her again: a life was such a short thing. All those things people carry, yet one day they would disappear, and so would the suffering inside them, and all that would be left was this. The trees, the moon, the dark."

Rachel Joyce, Miss Benson's Beetle

Contents

Preface

People often say, 'Why don't you write?' Over the years, I have replied in many different ways. Lack of time, lack of energy, lack of ideas. The truth is probably a mixture of these, and, as so often happens, life has always got in the way.

Now, due to a chain of complicated events, I find myself temporarily between homes and between jobs and living alone (except for my black lab, my boy) in a medieval borgo with a little time on my hands. So here it is: A collection of short stories with a twist, intended to leave the reader with a sense of frustration and *unfinishedness*. Be forewarned, I do not write for a passive audience! You must be willing to answer your own questions and overlook my penchant for split infinitives...

Martine Greslon-Collins has done much more than give me the use of one of her beautiful homes in Tursi, Basilicata (Italy's deep South) as the place in which to write this book. (I have taken time out to come here after many years spent in Liguria, a region in the North of Italy which captured my heart.) She has encouraged me and bestowed upon me such generous praise that my desire to write has been reignited.

I am living in an idyllic medieval borgo in a little stone house with beautiful views from the terrace of the oldest part of Tursi, La Rabatana. From the balcony, there are views of stone caverns, steep rocky hills dotted with trees and prickly pears and, on top, the 15th Century Convent of San Francesco D'Assisi. My only companions over the last months have been sheep, goats, feral cats and an assortment of birds: crows, cockerels, pigeons, owls and other birds of prey. And, of course, Martine.

Any recounting of Martine's life and her many talents would fall short of describing the

8

person she is. She is a friend. A versatile and unflappable chef. She is an expert on fine wines. A painter and decorator and furniture restorer extraordinaire. She is a boutique hotel owner in a wild and crazy part of Italy that is full of beautiful nature, beautiful people and copious amounts of chaos and confusion. She is able, if necessary, on the same day, to rustle up a buffet for thirty in celebration of the imminent birth of a friend's first grandchild. Then chop down one of the world's fastest growing plants under my neighbour's window, armed with nothing more than a tiny handsaw. Drive her trusty – if somewhat battered – VW off to the Hairdresser's to get her *barnet* done. Pick up enough bags of cat biscuits to feed her own cat and those in the vicinity (all named and cared for and lucky enough to eat said biscuits beneath the arches of her home, perhaps dreaming their dreams). Later, bring me round a jar of homemade marmalade and unblock my sink while I put the kettle on. Call in on her ninety-three-year-old neighbour and have a chat and a glass of homemade limoncello – and leave with a dozen fresh eggs. Yet, she is always home in time to make a three-course meal (with bread) to enjoy with her partner as they sip a glass of wine on the Arabic terrace of her home in La Rabatana which overlooks the Convent of San Francesco D'Assisi from a higher vantage point.

Faced with this crazy woman as a friend and this crazy place as a home, I have had no choice but to rediscover my enthusiasm for life and the love of words…

Given Away

Our father was a good-looking man. *Dapper*, some would say. Tall and dark and always immaculately dressed. On Saturday nights, he would play in a group, downstairs in a club on Queen Street. I'm pretty sure it was called the Crazy Hare, but my mother never mentions it now. He played the drums. I think that's why I love music with a beat. It's in my blood. In my veins. It's all about your DNA. Or, maybe, it's a memory from a previous life.

The group was called 'Simon and his Uncle', which I always thought was strange. Nobody in the band was called Simon, and none of them were uncles. Pat, Patrick O'Hearn, was a postman during the week. Nobody ever called him *Postman Pat* as he was retired by the time his namesake came along. He played guitar. Dave Redsmith was a window-cleaner who worked for his Cousin. He was a great singer but not much good at cleaning windows, according to Dad.

Grandma always said, 'Dave's a bad'un. A bad'un, he is.' She had a habit of repeating things as though she thought you hadn't heard her the first time. I don't know why they said Dave was bad. Something to do with the ladies on his rounds. Dave's brother, Eric, was on the keyboards. He was a quiet, nervous young man. 'As different from his brother as chalk and cheese. Chalk and cheese.' Grandma used to say.

When I was six, the band unexpectedly got their big break and left one Friday afternoon for Benidorm. They had a big blue van that Mum said wouldn't make it to Dover, let alone Spain. We had sausage and chips, and *scraps* from the chippy to celebrate. We had one sausage in three but it tasted so good. Mum showed us where Benidorm was on the map. I thought it sounded exotic. I imagined men with fine moustaches and black capes and women with red shoes.

'Simon and his Uncle' came back in late October. It was a school night but Mum let us stay up. She scrubbed our faces 'til they burnt and told us to put our best coats on. In the end we were late, and she made us walk quick sharp up the foggy lanes, then, cut across the fields to Fareston Garage. The van was already there but Dad wasn't in it.

Mum chatted to the driver for a while. Leaving us freezing on the forecourt. We lost the feeling in our fingers and toes and laughed that we could see our breath, white in the cold night air.

Suddenly, Mum took my hand and I took Sally's. Alice yelped as Mum grabbed her with her other hand and dragged us back the way we'd come. We didn't dare ask her where Dad was. We kept quiet. I think Mum wanted to get us home quickly and into our beds so she could get the cider out and have a good old cry.

The next morning she woke us up bright and early. Her hair was backcombed, her make-up on, the creases smoothed out of her skirt. She pulled all the curtains back and made us toast as though nothing had happened.

A few days later, she got a job in the chippy. Just part-time. We got free scraps and gravy on a Saturday night when she came home.

In July, Grandma Elsie died and we moved across town to live in her house. It smelt of old women and mothballs but Mum said it had an inside toilet and the smell of mothballs would wear off. She opened all the windows and scrubbed the floors on her hands and knees.

Mum had started having her hair done on Saturday mornings. She said Dad would come back for the funeral but he didn't. There were raised eyebrows and thinly sliced ham sandwiches after Grandma was laid to rest. Gran's sister played a couple of tunes on the piano and her Jack Russel, Jerry, joined in on the choruses. Then Dad's uncle, Harry, played the spoons on his knee and yodelled and the vicar was given a thimble of sloe gin when his Battenberg cake went down the wrong way. Mum said she couldn't bring herself to thump a man of the cloth on the back.

We started going to jumble sales and selling Grandma's stuff. It felt sad but at least we had a few days out. All those lovely old things that we were used to seeing when we went to her house on Sundays. Mum said Grandad had brought them back from abroad when he'd been in the navy. Grandad died before we were born. He got hit by a tram in Blackpool.

I liked all those old things in the house but Mum said it was tat and Grandma Doris seemed quite cheery to be selling Grandma Elsie's Persian rugs and jet necklaces and ivory elephants. The only thing Mum kept was a black lacquered jewellery box with mother of pearl inlay. She said it was Japanese and the woman on the front was a Geisha. I didn't know what a Geisha was. Mum said I could have the box when she died. I didn't want her to die.

Dad only ever came back once, to give our Sally away. Mum said he'd already given us all away a long time ago.

Derek

He was dead and gone and she tried to think of something nice to say about him. It wasn't easy. Well, he wasn't completely gone. He was on the mantelpiece in a black marble urn. She wasn't sure how much longer she could tolerate him being there as a constant, ever-present, reminder of all the bad times.

Thirty-seven years together and she'd stuck it out as she'd been brought up to do. Margery thought that God would compensate her for all the bad she'd endured. By the time she had realized that life didn't work that way, it was too late. Even now, the imaginary scales in her head would still jump out and catch her unawares. She was secretly still waiting for all the good to come along and balance out the bad.

But mostly Marge just trudged through life expecting the worst. A life that had never been lived. And now, it was too late. The funny thing is that she'd felt it was too late to change things for the last twenty years or more.

The kids had thought it a good idea to scatter Derek's ashes and had decided it would be fitting if she were to say a few words. She wondered why they had thought that was a good idea.

Initially, she had considered a passage from the Bible. Perhaps a couple of psalms. But Derek was not a religious man. He was a man who wouldn't have known a psalm from a salami or *his arse from his elbow* as Marge had often commented while he was alive. Though she couldn't say that now. She'd been brought up not to speak ill of the dead.

She'd looked online for a poem. Something profound and meaningful but nothing struck her as relevant. She sipped her tea and dunked a ginger biscuit thoughtfully. She realized that her only option was to write a poem herself.

She picked up the remote and turned off the TV, let the cat out and went upstairs to bed. Most nights she still woke up and, half asleep, stretched out her arm thinking Derek was still on his side of the bed. Then, she'd wake up a bit more and realize, with a sense of relief, that he wasn't.

Ever since dear Derek had departed, Marge had changed her ways. She'd taken to eating toast in bed in the mornings. Derek would never have approved of the crumbs. She had swapped watching boring documentaries about Bismark's foreign policy or Eisenhower's stance on science education, for cooking programmes. She liked the Jamaican chef who always wore a Hawaiian shirt and cooked tropical dishes on a beach in Wales.

Two days before Derek was due to be thrown to the wind, she ate her lunch on her knee instead of at the table (she was becoming ever more the rebel), and sat down to write her poem. She discovered that she was surprisingly good at writing poetry and started to consider a change of career.

On Monday, as they stood in the rain in their anoraks, Margery began to read the words that she had written. They were starting to wash away with the rain, so she read them rather more quickly than she had intended:

Well, Derek was a good man (we know that isn't true). He was a loving husband (if those here only knew). A good father to the very end and he'll be sorely missed (he was a shit-bag and a cheat and always bloody pissed). She turned the paper over and continued.

When she got to the end, Marge looked up and waited for the nods of approval. Too late, she saw their expressions. She would always swear blind that she had never intended to read the bits in brackets. Oh well, it was done now. She suggested going down the Horse and Dragon for a pork pie and a glass of cider.

Waiting

This is such a quiet place full of so many sounds. I put my head back, close my eyes, my face lifted towards the spring sunshine. There are cars on distant roads, a lonely sheep bleating. Wind rustling through grass and through leaves. There are birds twittering and birds chirping, and birds whistling and birds that cluck. A dog is softly whimpering.

It's getting quite late now and I'm still waiting for you to come home. Waiting to hear the sound of the gate opening at the end of the driveway. Waiting to hear the car engine and the tyres on the uphill track. I'm waiting to hear the car door open and close and the beep of the car alarm as you lock it. I'm waiting for you to come and hug me and spin me round the way you used to do a long time ago.

I'm waiting for you to kiss me when you come into the house. I'm waiting to sit down to eat together. I'm waiting for you to tell me about your day. It doesn't matter that you never ask me about mine or that you like to be waited upon. I've had a tiring day too. I'm waiting.

Then I remember that I am blind and you have gone. Nobody wants a wife who cannot see how important they are.

Call Me

She always says she'll phone tomorrow but she never does. I'm not sure whether to be upset that I've fallen for it again or whether to enjoy that moment of fleeting happiness in which I believe her. I know it's not her fault. I don't blame her. Children grow up. Grow apart. Leave home and start a new life. That's the way it should be. I'm happy for her. No. You don't understand. I really am happy for her. But it would be nice to get a call every now and then.

I haven't been out of the house for eleven days now. Sometimes I just can't face it. I get my shopping delivered. They ring the bell and leave it on the doorstep. I wait a while before I open the door.

Sometimes I wonder why I'm even here. What is the point? A lifetime of endless sacrifices. Of endless missed opportunities. Of endlessness.

For what? She doesn't care. I've heard it from her own mouth with that evil smirk on her face. *I'm not interested. I don't care.* Then you ask yourself where you went wrong. *What didn't I give her? Did I give her too much? I didn't give her a family but I tried. Does she know I tried?*

Then I finally get the call. But it comes in the middle of the night. While my brain is still asleep on the pillow, my ears are hearing things I could never have imagined, even on my darkest days.

I have no choice. I get dressed in the first things my trembling hands come across in the chaos that has become my prison: Black jeans, a denim shirt, a thick pink cardigan. I pull on the brown boots I find near the front door. I seem to be on automatic pilot now. I'm doing well. I've got this covered. I'm cruising at a speed of somewhere near blind panic. Bag. Phone. House keys. Car keys.

Car keys? Can I drive? Am I able, at this precise moment in time, to get into that heap of red and rotting junk parked outside my house and drive it to the Police Station? My heart is saying *No. NO. NO. NO.* I can't do this.

I put the key in the ignition and pull out. *Did I look behind me?* I don't know. It's dark. It's cold. There's nobody on the streets at four a.m. on a Thursday in May. People, normal people, are snoring peacefully in their good lives. Their pain-free lives. Their worry-free lives. At worst, they are bored. Give me boredom. Give me ground-hog day. Give me normality. Take me back to the days before all this.

The Police Woman (person?) on the desk has no expression. I give her my daughter's name. I speak to a detective I think that's what he said. I didn't catch his surname. Wilson? Benson? Watson? No. Not Watson. That *would* be strange. Elementary.

Water? He's offering me water? Water isn't going to make this any better. These aren't sorrows that can be drowned. He seems young. Too young to be doing this. Concerned. I nod gratefully and take a sip.

He's already telling me what has happened. What my daughter has done. My daughter. That part of me that I used to think was the best part. Blood of my blood.

A girl. She's hit a girl. With a bottle. Is she? I can't say the word. *Watson* says it for me. Dead. Yes. She is Dead. Last night another mother told her child to have a good time. Another mother is here somewhere, sitting in a cold room, wearing mismatched clothes like me. I feel guilty for thinking that there is some similarity between us. I hope *she* is not alone. I hope she has a good man by her side.

Then suddenly I'm retching. I make it to the sink just in time. Bile. Green bile. Again and again. I retch up the nothing that my stomach contains. I have no money for food. I have no money. Beans. Soup. My weekly shop.

My face is red from the slap of cold water on it. Somebody takes me back to *Watson*. He stands up as I enter. Concerned. Young. His chair scrapes on the concrete floor of the dingy room.

'When can I see her? When can I talk to her? What is going to happen to her now?'

Watson begins to tell me what happened. The odd word sticks in my mind: *Girl, party, taxi, street.* My head is spinning. I concentrate hard on not fainting. No more problems. A sip of water.

Dead. Dead on arrival at the hospital. An accident? No. No. Deliberate. *Why? Why would she do that? Drugs? My girl? My baby on drugs? No. No. That can't be. Positive? She tested positive? For what? Who is this child that came out of me and went into the world to kill?*

I remember when she lined up all her dolls in a row and kissed them all goodnight. I remember her in frilly white dresses. I remember her daddy throwing her up into the air and catching her. I remember the day he left and I know she does too.

That's the day she stopped going to church because that was the day she stopped believing.

I start to wonder if I should really be sitting here. She must be frightened. When I finally get to see her, her face is so white. Her eyes are reddish and darting. Darting from the table to the door. From the door to the table. We're both shaking. She doesn't look at me.

I suddenly realize that I should feel sorry for her but all I can think about is that other mother. I should stand by my only daughter and help her through this. That is what mothers do in films. She is mine. My blood. My responsibility.

I stand up and ask to leave. She looks at me then. That evil, spiteful glare. Her eyes are full of disbelief. *What kind of mother?* she is thinking.

A bad mother. A tired mother. I take a taxi home. I don't even consider driving. At home, I kick off my boots in the hallway. I crawl under the cold bedcovers, still wearing my clothes. I pull the duvet over my head and scream and scream and scream. Nobody comes.

Five Words

She pushed her huge bosom under your nose, said your name and asked you something. I don't remember what it was. I only remember the look on your face and the way you backed slowly away from her. It was obvious that you were torn. Torn between your desire to be worshipped by every woman in the village and your fear of the female form.

You've always preferred women who look like little girls; short, pencil-thin, long hair tied in a ponytail, and cutesy clothes. Each one the same. Another and another. As though you'd had a mould made which they all had to fit into. It was a bit more normal back then when we were young. But now it's... Well, I don't want to hurt your feelings but it is a bit disturbing. It worries me sometimes. When I think about it. Not that I do. Not often. I mean. How old are you now? Seventy? Seventy-one? Ah, sixty-seven? Really? Only sixty-seven. You do look older. I think it's your hairstyle – or rather the lack of one – and your clothes. I mean. You wear the same style of clothing as when you were a teenager. That's weird.

There's something a bit, well, sad really about not accepting your age. Embracing it. Living for the moment you're in instead of trying to recreate your past. Don't you agree? Hey, I'm all for freedom. You know me. Wear what you want. Wear what you like. But still. I can't help thinking it's sad to see an old man clinging so desperately to the past. A past that is long gone.

It wasn't lived? Yeah, of course I get that. You were too busy. You missed out on your youth. You had to work. I know. I know how things went back then. I think that what you did was honourable. It really was. A lesser man might have walked away and kept on going. Not you. I know.

No, no. Of course I'm not judging. Judgemental? Me? Come off it! You are joking, right? Well, yes. Yes. I guess you have a point. Walked in your what? In your shoes? What does that even mean? Walked in your fecking shoes. Hey, you're judging *me* when you say *I'm* too judgemental and you haven't walked in my fecking shoes have you? No. No. So shut it. Shut up!

So, you were backing away from that woman but she had no intention of giving up. She wasn't going to take 'no' for an answer, ha. It was so funny to see. She had you backed up against the railings with nowhere to go. And she said your name again and you looked right over the top of her head. You looked at some point far enough away on the horizon that you didn't have to look at those enormous breasts that she was shoving at you. And everyone around you was laughing. You thought they were laughing at you so I told you, 'No'. No, no. Somebody told a joke. It wasn't even funny but we were all in a good mood. We were all happy back then.

Anyway, I know you *knew* I was lying. They *were* laughing at you. Not in a nasty way. We weren't being mean. It was just so funny to see. There she was with her dress pulled down as low as she dare, and those great big breasts pushed up as high as they would go. And there you were. Frightened. Frightened of a pair of tits. You've got to admit that's pretty funny.

You know something? I think you're right. I *am* too judgemental. Mom used to say that. I judged people and I was spoilt and I was a martyr and I was selfish and I was... Can you even be judgemental *and* a martyr? I was only a little girl then. I didn't know what the word meant. I'm not sure I do now. What is a martyr? Do you think I'm a martyr?

She used to say some horrible things to me. Mom. Isn't it funny that I remember them all? No. No. I didn't mean it that way. Of course, it's not *funny*-funny. Did I tell you that when we were little, she used to get me on my own and tell me I was dirty and smelly? So, I had a bath every day. Sometimes two. And Dad used to go crazy about me using all the hot water. Do you remember?

Then she stopped talking to me. Just like that. I must have been eight or nine. I think we were still at the old school before we moved out of town. It was a couple of years before she died. One morning she came into the kitchen and I was making toast and she looked at me in that way she had. You know. That irritated expression she always had. Anyway, she turned to me and asked me if I'd *taken* a bath. Taken! Ha-ha. Yes, I swear she said *taken*. And I was quick at answering back in those days. Do you remember how quick I was? Anyway, I made a joke about it. I asked her why. I said, 'Why? Is there one missing?'

I know. Yes. I swear I really said that. I knew it was asking for trouble. Big trouble. I knew and yet, I said it anyway. And you know what? She stopped talking to me. Just like that. Just for those five words. I mean, what kind of a mother does that? She thought she was punishing me. She really did. But you know what? I didn't want to talk to her anyway. It was a relief. Yes, a relief. That's what it was. So, we lived out those last few years without ever a word exchanged between us. And do you know something? I was happy. I was really happy back then.

Missing You

They're not sheep. They're hedgehogs, he said. - They look like sheep to me. – You need glasses. – I have glasses. – Well, wear them then! – What for? To see the hedgehogs on the freezer bags?

She could feel another argument coming on. They always seemed to be arguing nowadays.

No. Damn it. So that you can see, full stop. You're just too proud to admit that you're getting old. – Old? Old? I'm thirty-seven. That hardly makes me Methuselah. – Who the hell is Methuselah? – I don't know. Some old guy from the Bible.

They looked at each other and started to laugh. Exasperated laughter. Liberating laughter. Long-overdue laughter. Tired laughter. The laughter of lovers, of accomplices.

Siena took his hand and led him into the kitchen where he'd abandoned the shopping. Sweeping aside the frozen peas and the tubs of salted caramel Haagen-Dazs ice-cream, he lifted her onto his mother's antique table and began to unbutton her blouse as she wrapped her long legs around him.

I've really missed you he thought later as they sat in the garden eating melted ice-cream.

Siena felt the warmth of the sun on her glowing skin and thought that it had been a good idea to bring the garden furniture out early this year. She took their empty dishes back into the kitchen and went back to sit a while with him before going to yoga.

He saw her look across at him and asked her what she was thinking. 'That I've really missed you', she lied.

Jam

Julia was fat. She'd always been fat. At school, they called her Jam Roly-Poly but as she grew up, that got shortened to Jam and somehow, it stuck. Her mother despaired of the cuckoo-child who struggled to survive in a family of tall, slim athletic-types. When her chubby pink cheeks turned out not to be baby-fat, Jam's mother secretly wondered if the hospital had given her the wrong baby to take home.

For as long as Jam could remember, her mother had looked at her as if she were something bought by accident that should really have been taken back and exchanged for something more suitable.

Jam's mother lay awake at night agonizing over the decision. She wondered whether to contact the hospital directly or whether to look for a lawyer.

Then, she realized that all she needed was a DNA test before she took the matter further.

She removed some hair from Jam's hairbrush and took it to her doctor. He explained that she would need hairs with a follicle and, it was impossible for him to tell. In any case, she would have to do the test privately. Saliva would be better. Jam's mother wasn't sure how to get a large enough sample of saliva.

Eventually, Jam's mother decided that it might be better to leave things as they were. She was not sure whether she could cope with the upheaval of exchanging Jam. Not because she would miss her, but because she would have to get used to the daughter that they would give her in exchange. Still, she was curious.

When Christmas came, she bought all the children a DNA kit, pretending that it was a way of finding out more about their origins and health. She didn't want to tell Jam outright that she hoped to prove that they were not related. It would only have caused an argument.

Jam's mother thought that if the test proved her right, then she would convince Jam to leave things as they were. She would be going away to university soon and that would be the end of it.

Jam decided not to do the test. She had been having similar thoughts to her mother. She had never felt like she belonged in this family but, as the relatives she had, had been such a huge disappointment to her, she really did not want to go looking for any more. She worried that she would not cope well with any more humiliation.

Jam didn't understand why she was so fat. At the breakfast table, her parents and her three brothers would tuck into a cooked breakfast of Cumberland sausages, smoked bacon, hash browns, fried eggs – one or two her mother would ask them

41

– fried bread and baked beans. Jam would look down sadly at her single rice-cake thinly smeared with low-fat spread. The same situation would re-present itself at lunch (a tub of low-fat low-sugar yoghurt) and at their evening meal.

Then, Jam wondered if exercise could be the answer to her prayers. She had always loved reading and watching films. Perhaps she should be more active.

On Saturday mornings, the boys used to cycle out to the stables on Primrose Lane and take their horses out. She'd asked her dad to drive her there so that she could try horse riding too. She didn't have a bike and, in any case, didn't know how to use one.

The stable owner had been a mean, pinched-faced woman. After much deliberation, she had brought out a slow, fat pony for Jam. Her jodhpurs were digging into the area where her waist should have been and rolls of fat were hanging over them.

When they had tried to give her a leg up onto the pony, she had been worried that they would drop her because she was so heavy. She was not frightened of getting hurt. She was embarrassed. Eventually, somebody brought a couple of little steps. Once back home, she had weighed herself and, upon discovering that she had put on a pound, decided that horse-riding was not for her.

Jam's mother sent her to ballet lessons but Jam couldn't get her leotard on and it had ripped at one of the seams. She'd locked herself in the bathroom, and cried and then she'd eaten the Mars bar that she'd bought with her pocket money. She had stuffed it all into her mouth so quickly that she couldn't breathe through the chocolate and caramel goo.

Jam gave up and dedicated herself to her studies. She was doing well at school where she excelled in Cookery. Her soups, pies and puddings always gained her a ten. Jam liked studying but she didn't like the other girls. They were mean to her.

Once, a group of them had invited her to the café after school. The other girls hitched up their skirts and folded them over at the waistband, took off their school ties and unbuttoned their blouses to show their inexistent cleavages. They stood in front of the mirrors and applied make-up.

Jam hitched up her skirt revealing her podgy knees. She unbuttoned her blouse to show her vest. Demelza Harrison-Smythe had back-combed Jam's hair and helped her put on lipstick and mascara. Then, blusher and black eyeliner. Jam thought she looked like a clown. The other girls said that she looked pretty.

At the café, one of the bikers had bought them all a coke. Jam was enjoying herself. Then, when she'd come back from the toilet to find a tampon in her drink, she had burst into tears and run out. The sound of the girls' laughter stayed in her head for weeks.

When she was thirteen, her mother got her a personal trainer, Gary. Jam had just started studying Nutrition and, with Gary's help, the weight had started to fall off quickly. She found that she loved running. She would run and run and never wanted to stop. She ran to get away from all the hurt and disappointment and there was so much of it that she ran an awfully long way.

At university, where she was studying Physical Education, Jam finally decided to do a DNA test. When it came back, she discovered, to her horror, that she had *not* been swapped at birth. Those awful people really were her parents and her brothers were her brothers. That is, *two* of them were. It turned out that Edmund's DNA did not match anyone in the family. The hospital had made a mistake and swapped him at birth. Her mother was distraught.

A Puzzle

There were an awful lot of pieces but somebody could have put them back together. Somebody with a lot of patience and a lot of time. Somebody with a table big enough. I could have become whole again. Once. Not now.

Too many pieces of me left with you. Then pieces of me left with him and most of the pieces left with them. Over the years. Slowly. One by one.

Some days – days like today – it seems that all that's left of the me that I once was, is the box. The empty box with a picture on the front that helps you understand where all the pieces go. The trick is to start from the corners and the outsides and work your way in. It's easier if you have an outline and then a closed space to fill in.

Even the box is tattered now. It looks like it's been somewhere cold and damp for a very long time. The picture isn't clear but I can make out a house in the country. There are children playing in the garden and a dog sitting under an olive tree sheltering from the sun.

In one corner, there's a woman with long dark hair and a beautiful smile. She seems strangely familiar. She's looking up into the eyes of a man who's smiling back at her. It hurts when I realize that the man is you and the familiar woman is me.

They are the 'us' that we should have been if we hadn't lost too many pieces.

The Eggs

My mother died and I had to go to the funeral. I had to pretend I was sad but I wasn't. Don't get me wrong. I wasn't happy. I'm not some kind of mean, crazy person. I'm not a monster. It's just that she didn't like me and I didn't like her and then she died and I tried to feel something *appropriate* but I didn't. You can't force yourself to feel something that isn't there can you? It's like trying to believe in God. When I was little, I believed and then I got older and I didn't believe and then there was a time when I really, really wanted to believe. But I couldn't.

There was a plaque on the wall in the hallway when I was a child. Gold letters on burgundy velvet. It read something like, *Christ is the head of this house. The unseen guest at every meal. The silent listener to every conversation.* It was at the old house near the park when we lived with Grandma. You've no idea how much that thing frightened me. I thought God was watching me everywhere. Even on the toilet. Yes. I know that's a thing now. I've got internet now. But back then I didn't know other people thought that too.

Anyway, when she died, I think the only sorrow that I felt was for Daddy. He really loved her. I never understood why. But he did. He loved her as much as any man could ever love a woman. I'd like to find a man who loves me like that. One day. Yes, one day I will. A good man. A man like my daddy. A man who takes care of me when I'm sick. He'll do the housework and the shopping. He'll cook me dinner and tell me I'm beautiful. We'll both go out to work and have lots of children. Like that actress years ago. I can't remember her name. I'd like to have two or three children and adopt two or three children and travel and do crazy things. I don't want a boring man who works in an office. I want real love. A man who'll look into my eyes when he tells me I'm beautiful.

Mom was a bit crazy when we were little. She painted the bathroom ceiling blue when she was expecting Freddy and Dad got so mad and stopped kissing her goodbye when he went out. Anyway, he stuck by her through it all. All the arguments and all the cheating. All the times she packed her cases and left us with Grandma and Daddy so she could go off with some man she'd only just met. At the butcher's or the baker's. I swear she would have just packed up her bags and left with a guy she'd met at the candlestick maker's if there had been a candlestick maker's shop in town. Daddy would always take her back.

I guess she was pretty back then. Before the accident. She had those big blue eyes and all that blonde hair that she pinned up every morning. And such a tiny waist. I don't think I've ever seen anyone with such a tiny waist. Like an hourglass. She had an hourglass figure. And I always got it wrong and said egg-timer. Well, it was an egg-timer. Mom used to use it to time the eggs. Poached or soft-boiled or hard-boiled for salads. She used to cut them with that thing that was razor sharp. I can't remember what it was called but I was always scared she'd cut my fingers off with it one day. She was crazy that way. You had to be careful. You never knew what was coming your way.

Anyway, when I was a little girl, I used to think she had an egg-timer figure and that made me think of egg cups and I thought of somebody with an egg cup figure and that made me laugh out loud. You know, the way you laugh when you're little. Not a care in the world. Only you have. You have lots of cares. But you don't know they're not important. Then you get older and get bigger cares and some people – not me – but some people, want to go back. Back to when they were little.

We had to make something at school with a hard-boiled egg once. I think it was hard-boiled or it might have had the insides blown out through a straw. I don't remember. I remember doing tie-dye eggs with onion skins or beetroot. Tie-dye. That was a thing in the seventies. Long hair and platform shoes. Yeah. The men too. Glam-rock. Good times. Dad had a Hawaiian shirt and he looked just like Elvis with his dark hair. All the women loved Daddy but he only had eyes for Mom.

Anyway, we had to do something with this egg. It must have been Easter. For school, it was. And Pete and Lucy and Daddy thought that I should do Humpty Dumpty. We made this wall and drew all the bricks and painted some cardboard green at the base. For grass. And a face. And, well, arms, I guess. And legs. Anyhow, we sat old Humpty on the wall and I went to bed happy. I can still remember how happy I was that night. Mom let me have some of her shoo fly pie.

The next day we packed Humpty up carefully and I took him to school and, you know what? There were so many Humpty Dumpties. I think half the school had had the same idea. And nobody cared but I felt so sad. I was really upset because I wanted a family with some imagination.

His

He used to hold her by the back of the neck. It was gentle enough to seem sensual, yet firm enough to worry her. A long time later, she would say that it was his way of telling her that she meant nothing more to him than any of his possessions. In fact, she probably meant less. She was something that he would keep for as long as it suited him. Something he would carelessly throw away when he had finished playing. She was his.

Fabio was a man who liked to play games. Thrived on them. Fed on pain. A man who never went for the jugular. He loved the thrill of the chase. He got a kick out of toying with his victims.

If his eyes were the windows to his soul, then he had all the shutters closed. They were black. As black as the darkest, moonless night that she could ever have imagined. If he had a soul somewhere in those depths, it was not on display. Not for her. Not for anyone.

He liked the fact that he could easily pass for Italian. She found that strange. Shouldn't a man be proud of his roots, of his nationality? For Fabio, Italy was synonymous with style and sexiness. With good food and good wine. Italy meant having the best and Fabio liked the best.

And yet, there were things that gave him away to other Italians. For one, he didn't love his mother. All Italian guys love their mother. But Fabio wasn't put on this earth to love anyone but himself – and some of his possessions.

He loved Bvlgari sunglasses and expensive shirts. Rigorously white. Rigorously long-sleeved. He wouldn't be seen dead in a short-sleeved-shirt. All his suits were Giorgio Armani. His cars were vintage or brand new and always freshly polished. He probably loved his cars more than he had ever, and would ever, love any living, breathing being.

Fabio worshipped his body and would lie in bed caressing himself. He loved the muscles he hadn't worked for and his flat, tanned stomach. He loved his smooth skin and his expensive smile. He adored the gold ring his father had given him, but not because it had any sentimental value. Sentiments *had* no value to him.

He owned a couple of buildings in the city and lived on the top floors of one of them. He liked to stand naked at the full-length windows, looking out across the flat roofs of the buildings below. She presumed it was one-way glass that you could see out of but not in. It wasn't.

Fabio liked the best restaurants. Tonight, they had a table booked – in his name – at Osteria Francescana. She wondered how he could afford this lifestyle and had once asked him what he did. She would never ask again.

He was a man who liked to give orders. He chose her clothes and underwear. He chose her perfume. He chose her bags and her shoes. He watched her dress while he lay on the bed stroking himself slowly. In her mind, he was not wholly human. He was part bird of prey waiting to swoop.

He told her to put on black, lacy underwear. Then he told her to take it off. He put his hand around her throat when he took her. She was frightened. She didn't want to stay but she was too afraid to leave. She hoped he would get tired of her soon. She didn't realize that her fear was what nourished him.

The 7.02 to Basingstoke

When my mother died, she was younger than I am now, though she looked older. She had perfect hair, her crowning glory. I later found out that it was an expensive wig. She had lost all her hair through shock and stress when the triplets were born. *They had a lot to answer for.* My mother's nails were always long and thick and so hard when they dug into my arms and legs. She ate a cube of jelly a day. She said that was the secret. She had a whole box of different nail colours but her favourite was pillar box red and, in summer, coral.

I never once saw her without make-up. Perhaps she slept in it and put a new layer on each day. Perhaps she got up early and crept into the bathroom to *put her face on.* I loved all those sprays and creams and bottles. I tried her eyelash curlers and her lipstick when she was asleep. My mother was almost always asleep. When she was awake, she watched TV or read stupid magazines. She didn't like me and made no secret of it. I was Daddy's favourite, taking all the attention away from her.

I never resented being hated by my mother. The feeling, after all, was mutual. I was old enough to understand that it was the way things were in our house. She loved the triplets and Daddy loved me.

One day, when I was older, she told me about the time that she'd tried to kill me. It was a shock but I didn't judge her. She had her reasons. Grandma had given her hot baths and mother's ruin and made her move the furniture around. I refused to budge. I always was stubborn. Whatever they did to try and kill me, I was there and I was staying. She probably remembered me in her prayers and asked for me to die. God wasn't listening that day. Praise be!

She told me that if abortion had been legal back then, she didn't know if she would have had one. I didn't know what I was supposed to do with that information. Whether to feel sorry for her or just accept that she needed to say it. I think it would have been worse if she'd told me that she would definitely have aborted me. I suppose I should feel grateful. I don't.

The strange thing is that the older I grew, the more I found her quite repulsive. Like a toad that a car has flattened in the lane. I thought of her as a slimy, smelly thing whose life ended with her entrails exposed for all to see.

My mother died very young. She was hit by the 7.02 to Basingstoke. She threw herself under it.

Paradise

April and Lucas were still considered newcomers to the village, though they'd lived in Castello Alto for nearly three years now. It was a beautiful house at the end of a medieval borgo on the road leading down towards the sea. Just far enough away from the locals to be private and give the impression that they considered themselves a cut above them. April always said that it had been worth the months that she had spent trawling through property ads and every weekend spent driving from their rented flat to go to viewings.

Lucas was often back in the UK promoting his books or away somewhere doing readings for his 'fans' so she'd seen a lot of houses without him. When she'd found this one, she'd been with her father and had immediately put in an offer. Lucas had been offended. Hurt even. He tried not to show it. The money was hers, or rather her father's. A late wedding present, his father-in-law quipped. April was the daughter of a Count. Lucas's friends had been impressed by that. His family would have been too, he imagined, but he was all alone in this world. He had a mother but they no longer spoke.

The couple had met at a party in Milan. Both had been 'forced' to go by friends. Neither of them was enjoying it. April didn't drink much or do drugs. She wasn't a party girl like her university friends. Lucas had only been in Italy for a few months and didn't really know the guys he was with. When he'd found one of them snorting something in the bathroom upstairs and another having a threesome in the bathroom downstairs, he had poured himself a drink and wandered out onto the dimly-lit terrace.

He was asking himself what on earth he was doing there and letting his eyes adjust to the lack of light when he'd spotted her. Tall, slim, with long dark hair tied into a tight ponytail which fell down her almost naked back, he had found himself staring. She must have felt his gaze on her as she turned suddenly and smiled. 'I'm sorry' he said in his English-accented Italian. 'I didn't mean to stare.' 'Yes, you did!' she replied in English, confounding and embarrassing him and making him laugh awkwardly. 'Well, you do have a rather lovely back', he tried to save the situation, grateful that it was probably too dark for her to see his blushes.

'Ah, only the back? The front you don't like?' she laughed. The truth was that he rather did like the front and also the impertinence of this Italian girl who joked with him in fairly good English. He moved closer to introduce himself but as he gazed into her chocolate eyes, something strange happened to his insides. The Italians refer to it as a *colpo di fulmine*, literally, being struck by lightning. It was love at first sight for Lucas. He wasn't sure, even now, if it had been the same for her.

As Lucas appeared to have (temporarily, he hoped) lost the ability to speak, April introduced herself and explained that her mother had been English. Lucas noted the 'had been' and felt an immediate sense of protectivity towards this beautiful stranger. She quite clearly was not in any need whatsoever of protection. She explained to him that *April* had been her mother's favourite month. And Lucas, somehow, managed to stutter out his name. She shook his hand. A gesture that he found both oddly formal and wonderfully electrifying.

They'd soon decided to leave the party and had gone to a little bar in a quiet piazza nearby. April told him that she lived in a small town on the Italian Riviera. Near Portofino, she explained. Lucas told her that he was in Milan with friends but lived in Bologna where he was teaching English at the University for a year. She liked the fact that he was so enthusiastic about his job and the place where he was staying. He was interesting and full of energy and very different from the boys she talked to usually.

Five years later and here he was, trapped in paradise. Married with a villa overlooking the sea and an odd assortment of ever-changing cleaners and gardeners, the servitù. Oh, and a baby on the way. His son and heir.

As he sat having breakfast on the South-facing terrace one morning, his thoughts were interrupted by April. 'What do you want?' she asked him. 'You are always unhappy.' It was not a question but he felt the need to reply. He knew it would have been kinder to deny it but it would also have been a lie. He didn't know how to make her understand that he wanted a simpler life. *Simpler than this? You have your meals made. You write. You travel.* She would always point out. Then he would feel guilty and ungrateful and that just made him feel even more unhappy.

'I feel trapped.' He said at last. Regretting it as soon as the words had left his mouth. April sighed. She didn't seem angry. She treated him like a spoilt little boy and perhaps, he thought, that was exactly how he was behaving. He finally had the chance to write and his books were doing well but, somehow, this life seemed to suck the passion out of him and his writing had become staid and predictable. Luckily, staid and predictable seemed to be popular with his readers.

April and Lucas didn't understand each other. She was always happy, especially now that the baby was on the way. He did try to explain his feelings but she never understood. He'd once said to her that he wanted to give up writing and go back into teaching. He missed his students. He missed the noise and the energy. He was not ready to grow old amongst the olive groves. He'd said to her that he didn't know what to write anymore. That he had no original thoughts. That everything had already been written. She had laughed out loud and told him how silly he was. She'd said that it was like saying that you're never going to speak again because everything has already been said. She didn't know that he was so unhappy that he would happily have stopped speaking too.

She always told him that he was too restless and he knew that she was right. But he wasn't willing to stop being who he was. He couldn't. He used every opportunity to get out and away from her and their enormous villa. Though the rooms stretched out over three impressive floors, he felt cooped up and claustrophobic wherever he went. He was trapped in a life that excluded him and made him feel lacking in purpose. Invisible. He felt invisible. And now there was a baby on the way and Lucas's restlessness was quickly turning into panic.

April called her bump *Lucasino* (little Lucas) and kept asking him to touch it. She wanted him to share her joy at feeling the baby move. He felt repulsed. He had a growing sense of dread which culminated in him coming to a rather unfortunate and untimely realization. He did not want this baby and he did not want his wife anymore. They would have to go. He was shocked at himself for even thinking such an awful thing but it was the truth.

You're Welcome

I'm glad I decided to invite you today. You looked stunning in that green dress. Your red curls falling down your naked back. I wonder how you manage to have a tan all year round living here. I never see you at the salon. Perhaps you go to some other place. Out of town.

The 'boys' took forever to get the barbecue going and I had to listen to you going on about curtain colours and colonial wallpaper. What *is* colonial wallpaper?

You said my hair looked nice today, with the emphasis on *today*. I hope that made you feel superior. I noticed you had lipstick on your teeth as I poured you another glass of wine.

You told me about Mick's new company car. I wasn't being mean. No. Honestly, I've never heard of that make before. Then you asked me if Annabelle had invited me to the coffee morning at her house next Friday. She hadn't, but then you probably knew that didn't you? Annabelle and I have gone our separate ways. I tried to tell her it was all a big misunderstanding. I would never. I mean. Brian? Please. He's not my type. Is he anybody's?

I did too much food as usual. You only picked at it anyway. Better to keep your figure and offend me than let yourself enjoy the day. Mick filled his plate for the second time and opened more wine. At least he seemed to enjoy himself. The afternoon passed quickly. I hope you both come round again. Maybe one day you'll tell me how you got those bruises.

It took you a couple more weeks. Nearly three. And then you told me. We were sitting in the main square outside the new ice-cream place. It's bright and breezy as they say and the ice-cream's so good but, do we really need another ice-cream shop? At first you were reticent. Unable to find a way to say what you obviously needed to. Then it all came flooding out. Once you started, there really was no stopping you.

He's violent. He gets drunk and takes it out on you. He's frustrated by your situation. *What situation?* It started with a slap across the face. It was so hard that you heard something click in the side of your neck and when you looked in the mirror in the Ladies room at the restaurant, you could make out the pattern of his fingers on your red cheek. The day after, it was black. He came into the toilets to tell you he was sorry. Knelt on the disinfected floor in his new trousers to beg you to forgive him. He cried. He said it would never happen again. He was so sorry. So sorry. He loved you. He had seemed ashamed. You had to eat your lunch with your back to the other diners. The waitress was young but discreet. She pretended she didn't know what had happened as she read out the specials.

When you got back home, he had said the sweetest thing. Something about having two lives so that you can do the right thing in the second one. You thought he was really intelligent and deep then. But it turned out it was just something he'd read.

Of course, he did hit you again. And again. Then he would turn up unexpectedly and start shouting about you cheating on him. He'd storm around the house looking for *him*. He even looked in the wardrobes. What was all that about? Then he'd kneel at your feet and cry and tell you how much he loved you. What a good woman you were. How he couldn't live without you. So, you forgave him.

Then he started asking you where you'd been and who you'd talked to that day and why the car was parked in a different direction. He started checking your phone calls and anything you wrote down. Checking the shopping list. Toothpaste, dishwasher tabs, mayonnaise.

He once saw you talking to the neighbour's gardener and threatened to shoot him. You were starting to get really scared by then. When you went out, you'd started looking at the ground.

I ate the last of my ice-cream feeling more and more alarmed. Mick seemed like such a nice guy. I couldn't imagine him being so paranoid or so violent. But, well, *closed doors* and all that. I asked you about the bruises and the black-eye behind your Gucci sunglasses. You'd threatened to leave him a couple of days ago. I see.

That's when I'd asked you if you were getting a divorce and you'd seemed so confused. 'Divorce? Of course not. Mick is the nicest, kindest guy I've ever met. Ok, a bit boring in bed. No, no. I'm not getting a divorce. I just wanted you to know that I've ended my affair with Jake. You're welcome to him hun. Your husband is a really nasty piece of work.'

Innocence

He liked to sit on the green bench on the corner of Honeydew Avenue, near the Newsagent's. Not every day and not when it rained too hard, but he was usually there in the morning. Early, so he could watch the children walking to school.

Most of the children were dragged along by their mothers. Some ran behind their fast-walking fathers. Some boys and girls would pass in little groups, chattering about this and that. He didn't remember their conversations or, if they were on the other side of the road, near the park, he couldn't hear them.

Then there was the little girl who always walked to school alone. He felt sorry for her. Her parents couldn't be bothered to take her to school and she couldn't have been older than six or seven.

She was a funny little thing with long skinny legs. She always wore dresses when the other girls wore jeans and t-shirts. A pretty little girl with blonde pigtails tied in bobbles.

That morning he didn't sit on the green bench. He waited in the trees for her to pass. She was alone as usual. Today she wore a yellow dress with white polka dots. It swished and swayed and showed her little knees as she skipped along. He touched himself in places that he knew he shouldn't and waited for her to get nearer.

She was surprised to see him there but looked up at him with such innocence. She didn't seem afraid. He asked her to go along the path to keep a look out so he could pee behind a tree. She took his hand and went with him.

The Cold Man

The day my second husband didn't come home from work, I pretended that he'd decided to stay on the train and go to Venice because that is what he always said he would do one day.

His dinner, an *arrosto di maiale* and potatoes made with garlic and rosemary fresh from the garden, was still in the oven an hour after he should have arrived. As I turned it off, I felt strangely calm, as though it were quite normal for an Italian husband not to return home after a long day in the office.

I got the girls ready for bed and read them a story from their favourite English storybook. It was about a Boxer dog who goes on a cycling holiday in the Lake District with a goat named Amelia. When I kissed them goodnight, neither of them asked where Daddy was. They were used to his absence.

He was the type of father who was absent even when present.

It was only when I sat down to watch the evening news at nine pm, that it occurred to me that I should probably let somebody know. I couldn't phone his elderly mother at this time of night. The Police? They would probably say that it was too early (that's what happened in films), and think he had gone off with the other woman. *Perhaps I should call the other woman.*

Half an hour later, I tucked into a dry pork roast with potatoes and downed a decent enough bottle of red wine then stumbled up the stairs to bed. I threw his pillow into the corner of the room. Put mine in the middle of the bed and slept soundly until the next morning.

It was Saturday. The sun was already high in the sky when the girls leapt onto my bed shouting, 'Mami, Mami. Can we play in the garden with Horlix?' I nodded slowly. My head hurt. I found my phone and called Elena. She was at the *parrucchieri* having her weekly blow-dry. Switching to her excellent, if heavily accented, English when she realized it was me, she immediately flew into a panic. 'What do you mean, *hasn't come home?*' Her voice was strained with anguish and I remember thinking, *that's how I should be feeling.* But I didn't. I was grateful when she ended the conversation quickly so that she could call the *Carabinieri.* I thought they were the military police but I happily left it to her.

Then I went into my enormous country kitchen, slipped a couple of slices of ciabatta bread in the *vintage* toaster and made myself a cup of tea. I had just enough time to eat my freshly buttered toast outside in the garden then get myself presentable before my Mother-in-Law arrived. Of course, in her eyes, I would *never* be presentable. I scrunched my eyes up against the midday sun. In the distance, beyond the olive groves, the sea was as calm and quiet as an artist's impression of June in Italy.

Elena arrived just before the two uniformed officers so there wasn't time to say much. I ushered the two men into the house and explained that I hadn't told the children yet. My Mother-in-Law had an expression like she was sucking on lemon sherbet. The elder of the two men nodded and made a note. They asked a few questions and I mechanically repeated what I'd already told Elena. Later, in Court, one of the officers would say I had been *cold and distant* and had shown little interest in the whereabouts of my husband. The expensive *avvocato* paid by Elena had objected to this. I had not. It was the truth.

As long as my husband was missing, the girls and I would sleep more soundly in our beds. No more raised voices. No more raised hands. No more threats. No more intimidating silences. No more mind-games.

The *Carabinieri* returned to the station in the next village. They left a card with the name and number of their *Maresciallo*. I would, they said, need to talk to him and make a statement.

I picked a few sage leaves from the pot near the door and began preparing sage butter for the *ravioli di zucca*. The girls came running into the kitchen to ask about the police and I told them that they'd come to talk to me because Daddy hadn't come home yesterday. All they said was, 'Oh'. I wasn't sure whether to feel sad that I had given them a father who meant so little to them or relieved that they were taking the situation so well. After a quick glass of lemonade, my younger daughter, Julia, did ask where her father had gone. They ran back out into the garden with the dog and carried on playing when I said I didn't know.

My Mother-in-Law, who had arrived in a taxi and a thick winter coat that she didn't remove despite the heat, sat rigidly at the dining room table refusing all offers of refreshment. I invited her to lunch and asked her to stay with the girls whilst I went to the station later in the afternoon. She looked pale and drawn. Filippo was her only son. I could not imagine her giving birth.

After lunch, I made coffee in my favourite mug - dusky pink with red hearts. The girls had given it to me one Valentine's Day. My husband had given me a designer bag chosen by his secretary. Elena refused coffee after having pushed her three ravioli round and round her plate with a fork and then left them. They were beneath her, as was the coffee, as was I. I felt sorry for her – occasionally.

The *Maresciallo* did not get up from his desk when I was shown into his office after a twenty-minute wait. I wondered whether this was a tactic or whether he was over-worked in this sleepy village. Not exactly a hotbed of crime. He was a middle-aged man without any visible signs of middle-aged spread. He sat tall and slim in his perfect uniform and silver-rimmed glasses. He didn't look away from the computer screen as I repeated my story.

'So, where do you think your husband is *Signora*?' he asked, suddenly fixing me with pale blue eyes. The question flustered me and, before I could stop myself, I had told him that he had always said he would stay on the train and go to Venice. It sounded ridiculous now.

'Venice?' the *Maresciallo* repeated, incredulous. 'The train to Rocca Malerba doesn't go to Venice *Signora*!' I explained that he could have changed trains or caught a different one from the city. I didn't know. That is how the search for my missing second husband began in Venice, 408 km away from us.

Back then there was very little CCTV and what there had been, or should have been, at various train stations, had been recorded over on a loop by the time the *Carabinieri* from Rocca in Basso had decided to contact their colleagues in the city and they had got around to sending somebody to check.

As I appeared to be their only suspect for now, I was given no information whatsoever as to how the investigation was proceeding. I saw the reports on the local news and, later, on the national news as the hunt continued. My Mother-in-Law kept me up-to-date. Though she disliked me intensely, she did not, it would appear, think that I had played a part in the disappearance of her son.

Unfortunately, the journalists were not of the same opinion. I quickly became the *English monster wife* who had killed her husband. My full-face photo began appearing in all the newspapers. It was almost summer break so I kept the girls at home. Away from spiteful and frightening comments. At least for now. For as long as I could.

Elena left to spend summer in her country home but telephoned me every day. My only other contact was with Clara, our friend and nearest neighbour. She was an excellent chef and brought us homemade rice salad and zucchini fritters, baked pasta and meatballs and other delicious dishes which we devoured gratefully. She told me that it was a pleasure as she had nobody to cook for now. Clara never mentioned my husband in front of the girls. I did not once feel judged by her.

Clara's own husband had been a violent womanizer. He had died suddenly of a cardiac arrest in his sleep a few years after we'd become neighbours. That's when she'd started babysitting for the girls and having the dog when we went on holiday. She wasn't much older than me and we'd become friends quickly, as often happens when you see your own pain in the eyes of another.

By Wednesday afternoon, it was the main story on the national news: Filippo De Maris, 37, husband and father of two young girls had gone missing on his journey home from work. Dr De Maris had a monthly pass but none of the ticket inspectors or the other railway staff could remember seeing him on the day in question. Several regular commuters were sure that they hadn't seen him either. (It turned out that several others were sure that they had.) He had also been spotted on a train going to Milan earlier in the day and on another going to Rome the day after. There were many more sightings when the story was transmitted on a television programme about missing persons the following week. A German tourist had seen him near her hotel in Venice, barefoot and begging for money. Thus, the search around Venice was amplified.

Six days later, I was called into the Station to answer more questions. I left the girls with Clara. She arrived with pistachio ice-cream and a ham-bone for Horlix. This time the *Maresciallo* wanted to know about my relationship with my husband. I told him, in broken Italian, that we had had a happy home life. That my husband had not seemed any more stressed than usual. That he had seemed perfectly normal when he had left for work that morning. That I had phoned him mid-afternoon to ask him to pick up fresh bread. That I had not been cheating on my husband. That my husband *had* been cheating on me since before we were married.

The *Maresciallo* did not seem surprised that my husband had a mistress. It was common practice here. He was, however, irritated that I had not mentioned this earlier. I told him, truthfully, that I did not know the surname of the latest woman – or rather girl. I thought she might be Russian. When she phoned to talk to him, I had noticed her accent. I gave him the names and numbers of the ones I did know about. I could see myself appearing more and more guilty in his eyes. Now, I had a motive for murder.

I didn't tell the *Maresciallo* that a few days previous to Fil's disappearance, while Julia was away on a school trip to Val D'Aosta and Arianna was being picked up from school by one of the other mums, Fil had taken me to a quiet bar by the sea. I'd felt excited about going out on a *date*. It had been a long time. I'd dressed in a pale silk dress and tied my hair back into a loose ponytail. Just a little cocoa butter on my lips. Fil always said my lips were my best feature, especially when I smiled. No jewellery, except for my grandmother's antique silver bangle and my white gold wedding band. Sandals and pale pink nail-varnish. I had butterflies, like before we were married. I was almost happy. Almost.

I'd even worn sexy underwear. I found it hard to feel sexy around Fil. He didn't attract me the way other men did. But I was making an effort. *For what? For the girls? For our marriage? For the family?* The plan had been to slip my underwear off before we left the bar and surprise him once we got home.

The evening did not go according to plan. Fil met me outside and walked into the bar before me, climbing the steps to a table overlooking the floor below. He sat down and studied his phone. I felt invisible. Everything he did was studied. When the waitress arrived, he ordered for us both. It wasn't a drink I would have chosen but I kept quiet.

As she turned, so did Fil and got a good look at her arse in tight black jeans. I felt embarrassed to be with such an insecure man. He always tried to spoil everything.

After our cocktails had arrived, he moved closer to me and whispered, in English, that he was having an affair and was leaving me. Leaving us. Leaving his daughters. He said it flippantly. As though it had been a snap decision. Not something he had thought much about. Her name was Julia (pronounced Yulia), he'd said and laughed when I'd flinched at him seeing a woman with the same name as our daughter. Suddenly, his hand was squeezing my knee. '*Niente scenate!*' he said. *Don't make a scene.* I felt suddenly nauseous and stood up to look for the Toilets. Once inside, I locked the door. Instead of removing my *perizoma* in anticipation of a night of passionate lovemaking with my husband, I threw my lunch up down the toilet bowl. When I came back to the table, he had gone, leaving me to pay for the drinks and get a taxi home. As I'd waited for it by the side of the road, a car drew up and asked *Quanto?* (How much?) Insult to injury, I had been mistaken for a prostitute.

Fil's first sexual encounter had been with a prostitute. A sex worker we would say nowadays. I don't think of myself as a prude but it had made me feel sick. Apparently, it was common here. *To learn how to do it I suppose. How sad.* I remembered having a conversation with friends once. All three of them had said they'd sell their bodies to get by if they had no money. I didn't tell them that I'd been in that position once.

My father's second wife had thrown me out of the house at just sixteen and he had done nothing to stop her. Out on the streets, I'd moved around sleeping on people's couches and floors. Friends and friends of friends. Until my aunt had found out and taken me in. Saved me.

At the time, it had never occurred to me to turn to sex work. I think I was too shy. I'd stolen food and money. *Is that more respectable? I don't know*. I'd been called a *Gypo* by a little girl once and looked away embarrassed as her father told her to 'shhhh'. My dress was dirty and I was rummaging around in a skip looking for something to sell. It had been a good day. I had found a teapot in perfect condition. I told the lady at Fallow's Antiques that it had been my grandmother's. I got enough money for a meal and a trip to the laundrette. A good day.

I had known rejection and had been on the verge of quietly accepting that of my husband. It did not hurt me when he described this woman to me. *She was younger and thinner.* So what? *She would be a better mother to the girls.* And that was when I changed my mind about letting him go.

This evening Clara came round with *lasagne al pesto*. She said it was no trouble. She'd had it in the freezer. The weather had gone unusually cool and she thought we needed some hot food. I hugged her and thanked her and invited her in to eat with us. She smiled and winked at me. She couldn't stay over. There was something else in her freezer that she needed to take care of.

Safe

The house she chose was no different from the ones on either side of it, yet something made her choose the one with the green gate. She walked up the path to the door. There was a knocker, no bell. She rapped it softly, then a little more firmly. The noise rang out in the silently dark evening.

It was snowing and she was wearing an old pair of pyjamas and slippers. She'd walked all the way across town and up the hill. Past the house she'd lived in as a girl. Past the park where she'd had her wedding photos taken. She was obviously in distress.

She couldn't feel her feet and had started shuffling along. Nobody had stopped her. Nobody had tried to help. The few people she had seen didn't seem to have seen her, and those who did had crossed the road to avoid her.

An elderly woman came to the door. She looked kind enough. She found herself being hurried inside, into a warm room with patterned wallpaper and a roaring fire. The woman gave her a mug of hot sweet tea and gently placed a blanket around her shoulders before she went back into the hallway.

Mary could hear her talking to the police on the telephone. She warmed her frozen fingers on the mug and sipped the tea. *I am safe*. She thought. The woman's husband came closer to her. He took the cup of tea from her hands and placed it on a little table near one of the armchairs. Then he started to fondle her breasts and push his rubbery lips against hers, trying to force his stale tongue into her mouth.

She turned and walked back out of the house. She felt safer in the dark.

Glorious

John Andrew Jackson had been asked to do a reading from his latest collection of short stories. He saw, with pleasure and a little alarm, that the crowd was larger than usual. John did not enjoy public speaking but if he were to sell his work, he had no choice. He opened the book on page 73 and began to read:

"The kitchen table was strewn with the remains of yesterday's breakfast, lunch and evening meal, plus snacks. Jilly surveyed it, horrified. There were so many empty boxes, packets, and tubs that it looked as though a family of four had been eating in her dingy, below-street-level apartment for at least a week.

There were three empty chocolate mousse pots, two plates covered in crumbs from the toasted baguette she'd eaten with lashings of salty butter. A whole baguette just for breakfast. She licked her lips as she remembered how delicious it was to have greasy butter dripping down her chin and then to lick it off her fingers.

She found a bag and gathered up the seven empty, family-sized crisp packets and the empty boxes of custard creams and ginger snaps, dividing them up, ready for collection. She wondered what the refuse collectors must think. Or her neighbours, who knew she lived alone. They were probably busy people who didn't even notice her. Normal people.

Jilly went back to the table and cleared up the empty bowls that had contained cornflakes, sugar and milk or chicken soup or noodles. She put them in the dishwasher. Then she checked the two pizza boxes to see if either of them contained a slice of meat-feast pizza that she had overlooked. They were both empty. Not even a crust.

Today I'll start my diet she thought. Then added, *again!*

It was already a quarter past eight. She would be late for work. Luckily, the office was only a two-minute-walk away. Twenty minutes later, she was washed, dressed and ready to leave. Everything was tidy. Everything was under control.

On the way to work, she called in at Jake's Bakes and bought a box of a dozen assorted cream-cakes. Mainly sticky chocolate eclairs and squishy sugary doughnuts. 'My turn to take the cakes in today', she explained to the girl on the till. She wasn't listening. She wasn't interested. She'd heard it all before.

A few minutes later, Jilly sat down on her usual bench. It was starting to rain but she hadn't noticed. She was licking creamy custard, from her third vanilla slice, off her sticky fingers."

John felt a little deflated. He really wasn't keen on this story. All of his stories were somewhat sad but this one was awkward and depressing. He wasn't sure that his agent had been right when she'd told him to leave it in.

The audience applauded and seemed to have appreciated it. Picking up their various bags and scarves, and umbrellas, they were starting to make their way towards the light buffet with drinks. He usually found that, when he read from this story, people avoided the snacks.

He turned around, looking for the woman who had organized the evening, Yvonne. Instead, he came face-to-very-pretty-face with the girl who had been sitting in the middle of the front row. She had a glass of white wine in one hand and a plateful of sausage rolls, sandwiches and crisps in the other. 'Nobody seems to be hungry tonight. All the more for me!' she shrugged. John recognized her lovely Irish accent and asked where she was from. She told him she was a Galway girl. 'For my sins.' She added. John immediately began to think about sin. Not the sin of gluttony from his story but that of lust.

As he imagined this nameless Irish girl completely naked in his bed, he suddenly realized that she was talking to him. She was complementing him on the unusual story and the fact that he often used the female voice. His female fans did seem to find this intriguing.

'As you can see, *I* have a healthy appetite too,' she joked, nodding at her plate. John was still imagining her naked and was now wondering about her *sexual* appetite. The girl, who later told him that her name was Annie, took his distraction for lack of interest. She was making to leave, when John suddenly blurted out, 'Would you like to go to a hotel with me?'

Annie laughed and told him that she was a huge fan and was so happy to meet him at last. John blushed and wondered if he had really said those words aloud. Perhaps he had imagined it.

A small group was forming, and reluctantly, he had to leave Annie and answer a few questions and sign copies of his book. He gave them his distracted attention, though they didn't seem to notice, then went to thank Yvonne.

It was getting late and he was hungry. Almost everyone had gone so he said his goodbyes and walked out into the carpark. It was dark already and the air was fresh. He took deep breaths as he headed towards his car. When he reached it, he found Annie leaning against it.

'Yes.' She said 'I'd love to go to a hotel with you.' John blushed again as she pulled him towards her. They did not go to a hotel but had sex in the back of his car.

'I'm married.' John said afterwards, pulling up the zip on his black jeans. 'I know.' She said, 'but it's too late now.' She laughed as she pulled his zip back down. The second time was slower, less urgent, but just as passionate.

The Wife in the Wardrobe

My wife is beautiful and such a bitch. When I look at her, I want to buy her flowers and kick her in the stomach until she screams. She is exactly what I thought she was when I married her and everything that I despise. She is sprawled on the bed, her face completely covered by that long, red hair. For a moment, I think about taking off my jacket and tie. Instead of going to work, I could take the kitchen scissors to those curls while she sleeps peacefully. The sleep of the guilty who could not care less.

I have not caught her out yet, but I will. That curve below the curve of her perfect breasts contains the proof of her crime. I know she has been with him. I can smell him on her. She is happy. He makes her happy. I imagine them together laughing at me, the pathetic loser who would bring up another man's child rather than let people know that his wife has been unfaithful.

We have another scan on Monday. I hope that bastard child is dead. Dead inside of her. I imagine her pain when the doctor tells us. I imagine her pain as she realises her plan has not worked. She will not get my money. I'll make sure they don't get a penny. I'll throw her out on the street. I tell her if she tries to leave, I'll ruin her. That she'll end up without a roof over her head. I tell her that I'll find someone younger and slimmer and cleverer than her. She laughs. She is not afraid of me. Bitch with that thing inside of her. Swelling like a forgotten ball of pizza dough. At night, I wake up sweating and shouting. I dream that I have cut the bastard out of her and it is a girl. It wraps its little arms around my throat and calls out, *Daddy! Daddy! I love you, Daddy. Please don't kill me.*

She's sure it's a boy though. She has already chosen the name. She's going to name him after her father. *A good man*, she says. She always makes a point of letting me know this, so that I know that I am, by reflection, a *bad* man. She wakes and asks me what I'm doing. I ignore her and look at my phone. Jessica has already sent me four messages and it's only twenty past eight. She'll have to go. Not that I'm worried. It's easy enough to find another whore. Another bitch to spread her legs for a free meal and a designer handbag. I've started thinking about the new office girl. What's her name? She wears those tight black skirts and low-cut blouses for me. Always laughing and twiddling her hair and running her tongue over those raspberry-crush lips when she brings letters in to sign. One day I'll lock the door and bend her over my desk. My phone pings. Another message from Jessica. I look at my Rolex. There's time to call in on my way to work. I'll park the Maserati up the hill behind the school so the bloody nosey neighbours don't see it. God, I hate living in this village. Her idea. Her fault. Bitch. Now she wants to move into the city. *It'll be easier for child-care*

103

she says. *I'll be able to go back to work*, she says. Ha! Where does she think she is going? Nowhere. She is going nowhere.

Jessica is waiting for me in a satin kimono-type thing. She thinks she's sexy. Stupid cow. I don't care about her clothes. I want what's under them. I pull it off her and see she's wearing a red bra and thong with her high-heels. Such a cliché. *Yes Jessica, you really will have to go*. But, one for the road won't hurt, will it? "Take them off!" She looks hurt. "Take them off NOW!" I yell at her. She doesn't move. There is a flash of defiance in her eyes that is quickly replaced by fear. I can smell her fear. It only takes a moment to throw her onto the sofa in the hallway, rip off that stupid red material and take her. Take her. She is mine. Pathetic bitch, how dare she cry? I tighten my grip on her throat. She stops struggling. Whore.

It's Monday, another scan. The receptionist at the Doctor's has enormous blue eyes. Whenever she sees me, she starts fluttering those long, dark lashes at me. I'll probably phone her in the afternoon. Take her to *Il Galletto* for lunch tomorrow. They know which table I like. Quiet. Good Italian food and wine. It makes me smile that it's my wife's favourite restaurant. The owner is discreet. I'm there on business, of course. A receptionist couldn't afford to eat there unless her Sugar Daddy was paying. I shudder as I think of the word *Daddy*. I'll listen to her going on about her job and her flatmate and pretend to be interested. A few nods in the right places and she'll drop her knickers in the car for me. She looks the type. I might ask her to go into the Ladies and take them off before we leave. She has a look of those brainless slags I used to have in the back of the car when I was younger. One after the other. All the same. Dirty whores. They're all married with kids now. Fat and ugly. I saw one of them on Facebook. Fat bitch has a brain tumour. She's really let herself go.

The Doctor arrives. A leggy blonde in a tight white lab coat. Not much make-up. A fresh, flowery smell as I brush past her into her office. She crosses her legs behind the desk and looks at my wife's details. I wait while they go through to the scan area. When they're ready she calls me in. 'You can come through now *Daddy*.' She smiles at me and I realise she has freckles. I've never noticed them before. Cute. She says something about the baby but I'm looking at her arse through the white coat. I imagine it firm and pert. She's a bit meatier than my usual type. She must be in her thirties. A bit too old for me and yet. There's something about her. The thought that she spends her days with her fingers inside other women gives me a sudden hard-on.

Doctor Elizabeth Mason-Howell gives us the *good* news. The baby is perfectly healthy and growing well. All the measurements are good. Do we want to know the sex? My wife looks at me to see how I feel. *How do I feel? I feel like I'd rather be in a king-size bed with Doctor Elizabeth Mason-Howell running my hands over those hips and finding out if she knows as much about men's genitals as she does about women's.* Her lips look so soft. I imagine them tight around...

'Amore?' My wife is half Italian and loves throwing in the odd word. She always calls me *Amore* in that stupid high-pitched voice. Silly cow thinks she's clever because she has a degree in languages. She should try going to a real university and getting herself a real degree like mine. 'Do we want to know the sex?' she asks. *Do we? Do I? I couldn't care less what sex her bastard child is.* I smile and say, 'Of course, darling.' Doctor Elizabeth seems so happy that *we* are having a boy. My wife is smiling. Satisfied. She was right. She is always right. It's a boy. He is due in October. I can't remember the exact date Elizabeth gives us. I'm distracted by my erection. I say I need to smoke and go and ask *blinking blue-eyes* where the toilet is. Then I have a couple of cigarettes outside in the spring sunshine. The kids are coming out from the college across the road. The girls, giggly and innocent are so delicious braving shorts and tight tee-shirts.

We're waiting for the train back. I told her we couldn't go by car as there was no parking. Stupid cow believes anything I say. It's a 'high-risk' pregnancy. A few spots of blood at the beginning and Elizabeth signed her off work and told her to rest as much as possible. Yeah. Sure. I'm going out to work to keep her and her bastard while she lays in bed all day, stuffing her face and phoning her lover. I'll find out who he is. She thinks she's clever but I know that thing isn't mine. I imagine them laughing at me and planning how they will be together after the baby is born and she's got a divorce. He's there on the other end of the phone thinking of all the money his son will bring with him. He's always wanted a boy. He's dreaming of taking him to boxing matches and kicking a football around the garden with him.

When they manage to get their hands on maintenance money for the little bastard and her half of all I own, they'll rent themselves a nice little cottage by the sea.

'So?' she asks. 'Are you happy that it's a boy?' I look round at her with disgust on my face. Surely, she can see how I feel about her! 'It doesn't matter,' I snap. 'Let's hope the next one is a girl.' I hear a sharp intake of breath but she doesn't have time to reply. The train is pulling in noisily to the station. The next one, ha! There will be no *next one*. I just said that to hurt her. She has always been so sensitive but more so now with that bastard inside her. She looks out of the window at the passing hills and trees. She is crying. I smile and look at my messages.

It's a Thursday morning in early August and I'm getting ready to leave for a *business trip* to Venice. The bitch is sad. She wants to come with me. She loves Venice. She enthuses about the architecture and the food. All she thinks about now is stuffing her face. Yesterday she wanted me to pick up Kentucky Fried Chicken on my way home from work. Such a shame that I forgot. She was *really looking forward to it*. There was nothing ready. *Could I make some pasta?* Could *I* make some pasta? 'I've been at work all day not lazing around in bed stuffing my face with chocolate eclairs and Pringles! *No. I can't make some pasta. Make it yourself you lazy cow!* I'd snarled at her.

She comes to the door with me now and tries to kiss me goodbye. '*Buon viaggio!*' I can't stand it when she speaks Italian. Silly cow. I mumble something about seeing her soon and close the door on her. I put my case into the boot and check my phone before I drive away. She has come out into the garden and is waving at me. What a state in her dressing gown with her hair all over the place. I hope the neighbours haven't seen her. I smile to myself at the thought of the flowers that

I've ordered for her. They should arrive mid-morning.

My husband is a busy man. He's always at work and when he isn't, he's on the phone. His clients call him and send him messages at all hours. I feel so sorry for him. He's just left for a business trip to Venice and I know he really wasn't looking forward to it. I waved him off from the garden of our four-storey house, the nicest house in the village, then rushed to one of the five bathrooms to throw up. I wonder how much longer I'm going to be in this state. I'd like to go into town and buy some bits for when the baby arrives. The baby. My baby. *Our* baby. I run my right hand over my bump and feel so blessed. A boy, Ben. My folks are so excited about their first grandchild. They're flying back from Portugal a few weeks before the birth.

The loud buzz of the intercom makes me jump. I wonder if there's a way to turn down the volume. It always seems to echo through this big old house. I can't see the delivery guy for all the flowers that he's holding. I take some off him and put them on the Louis XIV desk near the front door. 'There are more,' he says, heading back to a white van parked outside the gate.

All together there are seventeen bunches of seventeen yellow roses. I stick them in the double sink with some water while I hunt around for vases. Seventeen is an unlucky number in Italy and the flowers are yellow. My husband must have forgotten that I hate yellow flowers. Such a shame. All that money. It is so kind of him but I would have preferred a single bunch of those great big coloured daisies. It amazes me that my husband seems to know so little about me. It must be because he's so busy with work poor darling. But things will be so much better when our baby arrives.

I have a great time away with Doctor Elizabeth. Silly cow wants to go out and see

Venice. Go out on a gondola. What a cliché. Wants dinner in one of the trattorias. Wants to see glass-blowing. Christ on a bike. I want her in the hotel bedroom. Nothing more. We're not on honeymoon. Silly cow. I start to regret not having brought *blinking blue eyes*. I give in and take the slut out to dinner. It's a lovely place in the corner of an open piazza. There is piano music coming from one of the open windows nearby. A girl in red heels clickety-clicks her way from one corner of the square to the other. I watch the swish of her skirt and am aroused.

The food was good. Surprisingly, the conversation too. I'm getting a few jealous glances from the guys at other tables. But enough now. I pay the bill and try to take the good Doctor back to the hotel. She wants to go for a walk. I agree. It's romantic here by the canal with domes and bridges in the distance. I push Elizabeth up against a wall and kiss her. She has beautiful eyes. I could look into those eyes forever.

We go back to England the following morning. I know this sounds crazy but I've decided to divorce my wife. I'm going to ask Elizabeth to marry me. I can see us living together somewhere on the South coast. She can continue working so that I can listen to her talking about her patients and what she has to do to them. I will retire. I've had enough of being in the office.

When we get back to the house, Elizabeth waits in the car. The house is empty. The bitch must have gone to be with the father of her bastard. I call Elizabeth in. I want to take her on the bed I share with my wife. It is delicious. The best sex ever. I am so excited about our future together.

Suddenly, the wardrobe door opens. I can't help but scream. I don't have time to feel embarrassed though. I realize that my wife is in there with her phone. She has made a video of us. 'Surprise!' She looks so smug. Doctor Elizabeth looks shocked. My wife is laughing.

The bitch asks for a divorce. Adultery. The DNA test proves the baby is mine, so that's me in the shit for the next twenty-plus years. I console myself by taking Elizabeth out to lunch as soon as things have died down a bit. The engagement ring is in my jacket pocket. I wait for her at the table, planning what I will say and checking there is enough room to get down on one knee. She is a little late, probably tied up with a patient. I imagine her with her fingers inside one of her pregnant mothers and 'am aroused again. Our future is going to be oh so rosy. I check my phone. No messages.

The restaurant door opens and two women are shown to the next table. They are laughing and chatting. One is a pretty blonde, the other is heavily pregnant but is still beautiful. They toast each other with a glass of lemonade. 'Here's to cheating husbands' my wife says. Elizabeth replies, 'and here's to the wife in the wardrobe!'

The Haven

The only thing left was a clock, hanging above the kitchen door. It had stopped ticking weeks ago at 7.40, or thereabouts. It was one of those clocks without numbers. She had no need for precision. Time had become approximate. The minutes didn't matter now. Nor the hours, nor the days. It was all just... passing.

When she closed her eyes at night, she prayed to open them in the morning and find that all this had gone away. She was always disappointed. They had come to this place full of hopes and full of dreams but now they were all gone. The others were all dead. Her beautiful Lottie, white and blue and cold and dead on the floor.

She wondered why she was still alive. Why the poison hadn't killed her too. Perhaps it was just a matter of time. The men came back every three days or so and stayed overnight. If she let them enjoy her without protesting, they would give her food. Sometimes just a few crusts and some cheese. Once, the older man with the limp had given her a bowl of pasta. The smell made her mouth water and the saliva drip from the corners of her mouth but when she'd tried to eat it, she couldn't seem to swallow.

Lottie had brought her here to this place, The Haven, high in the hills. The rooms were beautiful. The views were stunning. They sat out of the terraces and enjoyed the silence. Then, something had gone wrong. They had got sick. *And now? Did they intend to keep her in this non-existence? Would she be set free if she survived? Would they sell her or kill her or just keep her here and use her.* The questions ran through her head on bad days. On good days, her mind was blank.

The cramps started again and she ran down the corridor, not thinking of her nakedness. She threw up bile, green and watery. There had been no food for days. The men must be due back soon. She would be good this time.

For Obvious Reasons

Are you ok?

> Yes, fine. You?

Yes. You aren't very chatty.

> I don't like texting. I'd rather phone you.

I can't today.

> Because your wife is there?

Wife????????!!!!!

> Well, whatever. Acquaintance?

You've been together for eleven years. What should

> I call her?

I haven't decided if I like her yet!

> Is that supposed to be funny?

There was nothing funny about their current situation. At least, not for her. He had been her first love at university and she had been his. Then, they had met by chance twelve years later in Italy. What were the chances of that happening? To her it was destiny. To him, it was difficult. He had never been good at making decisions. He couldn't leave his partner, Melinda. He was not one for upheaval.

Jess had been looking out of the window while she washed dishes in the hotel where she worked part-time and, suddenly, there he was. She'd recognized him immediately. Her boss had told her that a group of cyclists from England had checked in the previous afternoon but she had never dreamed that one of them would be Charlie.

He was as tall, dark and handsome as ever. And now he was also tanned and super fit. She wondered when he had got into cycling. He'd been a bit of a lout at uni. Then again, this was the first time she'd seen him in Lycra. Black and lime green. It suited him. As she stood staring out of the window at him, he looked up from checking his tyres. She thought he'd seen her but he was just gazing in the vague direction of the hotel. Their eyes could have met across an Italian terrace, but it was not to be.

Her boss, Rosa, came into the kitchen in her wheelchair and started checking the bookings on the computer. Jess went over and hugged her. She was such a kind woman and had become a good friend. Despite all her health problems, she had been there for Jess when her husband had left her unexpectedly. She had been pregnant with their first child. Rosa had offered her a job, taught her the *tricks of the trade,* like how to make a delicious ragù, and helped her study Italian. The locals had taken some convincing that a Scottish girl could make Italian food but they were beginning to accept her as one of their own now. Jess asked Rosa about the cyclists and found out that the group had cycled from France and was only staying a few nights.

After she had finished off in the kitchen, Jess drank a quick espresso with Rosa and then went home to let the dogs out, catch up on a few chores and get ready for her evening shift at the hotel. She would be serving at tables well into the early hours and then cleaning the kitchen again. She wanted to have a shower and do her hair and look nice for when she saw Charlie. She was excited now at the thought of catching up on his news. She found herself wondering if he was single.

Back at her little yellow house on the hill, Jess flung open all the blinds and the French doors onto the terrace so that her dogs could have a run around. Her *motley crew* as she called them. There was Waffle, her husband, Maurizio's dog and a Labrador-cross puppy, Hash. The newest arrival was Cole, a boxer, who was nearly eight, all rescued from the local shelter. The villagers joked that she would soon need a bigger house or a smaller heart.

The late morning sun came flooding into her home and, even after all these years, she smiled and marvelled at just how beautiful it was. Beryl the kitten stretched herself out in the sun and then wrapped herself around Jess's legs as she tried to carry her plate of salad out to the little round table on the terrace. She was not a cat person but Beryl had adopted her. The dogs either liked or tolerated her so, for now, she was staying.

Jess looked down the hill at the terraced strips of grass cut into the land. It was so peaceful and secluded here. The dogs were running through the olive groves, sniffing the little blue flowers on the rosemary and chasing still sleepy lizards along the low stone walls. Life had been hard since Maurizio had disappeared but she had rolled up her sleeves and made a life for herself and she realized that she was happy.

Jess allowed herself an hour to sit out on the terrace and enjoy the early summer sunshine. As she sipped her juice, her mind began to wander. She thought about the happy, carefree years she'd spent with Charlie. They say you never forget your first love. She wondered if Charlie still thought about her.

Their relationship had ended when he'd gone to do his PhD in London. They had tried to carry on but the long distance, the lack of time and the very different lives they were leading, meant that they had both concluded, reluctantly, that it wasn't working out. Everyone thought they were that golden couple who would always be together. Charlie and Jess. The perfect combination. Like cheese and onion. *You are the onion*, Charlie had joked. And she'd laughed and called him cheesy.

After a lovely cool shower, Jess pulled on button-up beige jeans and a fresh white t-shirt; smoothed her hair back into a high ponytail and put a touch of pink on her full lips. She didn't usually wear make-up in summer. It was too hot. A few leather and cotton braids around her wrist, her comfy silver sandals and she was ready. She said her goodbyes to the motley crew, smiling to herself at how silly she was, and set off on foot along the narrow lanes. It was a longer route but it was cooler and quieter and she had plenty of time.

She walked along breathing in the fresh air coming up from the sea and taking in the view of little houses covered in bougainvillea, of palm trees and huge cacti and, of course, olive trees as far as her huge green eyes could see. She watched the lizards darting in and out of crevices in the walls and butterflies fluttering on the slightest of breezes. She said *Buongiorno!* to the occasional tourist, usually couples or small groups on hiking holidays, and stopped and chatted when she saw someone she knew.

Sometimes Jess got distracted by so much beauty and thought that her life was pretty perfect. Then she was jolted back to what had happened to her only three years before. Her beloved Maurizio had gone out on his scooter one morning and had completely disappeared. His last words to her had been, 'I've got to go now'. Search parties had been sent out. He had been seen in the village buying bread but then, nothing. Everyone in the surrounding area had joined in the search. Maurizio was from Pisa and he and Jess were new to the area but everyone adored him. He was so kind it was impossible not to. He was always happy, always willing to help anyone in difficulty. His disappearance baffled them all.

Jess had been expecting their first child, a boy. She had known it would be a boy. A Christmas baby. They were so happy and excited. It didn't make any sense that her husband should just disappear. Jess had been distraught. She had stayed in bed and cried and cried until she could hardly breathe. She had stopped eating and was getting weaker and weaker. When she fell asleep, the nightmares came and she saw her husband dead at the bottom of the river or living a new life in the city. She would wake up screaming. She went for her next scan alone and in tears and was told the terrible news that the baby's heart had stopped beating.

Her husband had gone. Her baby was dead. Her life seemed so painful that it did not seem worth living. She felt an overwhelming sense of guilt for not having saved her baby. Everyone had told her to eat, to think of the baby but she hadn't been able to. The doctors assured her that it was not her fault but she didn't believe them. She grieved for her husband without knowing if he was dead and for the son she felt she had killed. Later she would feel so angry at Maurizio because, if he had been there for her instead of disappearing, she was sure things would have been different.

She grieved for what could have been. For what should have been. She imagined Maurizio rubbing her aching back and going with her to antenatal classes. Touching the bump which would soon have been their baby and feeling him kick. She imagined the birth of their baby with her husband holding her hand and helping her to breathe. She imagined Maurizio proudly holding their son. She imagined how excited he would have been coming to collect them from the hospital and take them home to their little yellow house on the hill. She imagined the happy family she always thought he would have given her and she was angry with him.

Then, she had met Rosa. Rosa came and brought her food every day despite her own health not being good and despite the awkwardness of the wheelchair. She never missed a day. She would chat to Jess in her cheery Italian and over the months Jess began to heal. Slowly. Very slowly. But Rosa knew that she would be okay.

When Jess took in another dog from the shelter and started caring for her garden again, Rosa knew that she was ready. She offered her a job as her right-hand-woman at the hotel. At first Jess had refused, as Rosa knew she would. Gradually, though, she had realized it was the right thing to do. She needed to work and she needed to get out of the house and be around people. Nowadays, Jess was as much a part of Villa Rosa as Rosa herself.

The church clock struck four as Jess walked across the village square. Perfect timing as always. Rosa was outside laying the tables under the pergola. She worked slowly, methodically, hindered by the wheelchair and the weakness in her hands and arms but insistent on doing the job herself however long it took her. She had been an inspiration for Jess when she had needed her most and she still was.

Rosa moved round and round the tables smoothing out the crisp white tablecloths. Everything had to be perfect. Then she went back inside and got the napkins. 'Well don't just stand there!' Rosa said in her heavily accented English. Jess laughed. She had been caught out. Rosa told her to get the ragù ready and, once it was simmering, to make a start on the antipasti. *Yes, Boss* Jess thought, smiling to herself.

As Jess was in the kitchen chopping the carrots, onion and celery for the *soffritto*, she heard Rosa talking to the cyclists outside. She rinsed her hands and went to the back door. Too late. The boys had gone to their rooms. They would probably be showering after the hard day's cycling. She smiled to herself at the thought of all the times she'd showered with Charlie. Rosa caught her out again, looking at her inquisitively. She would explain later. She was busy.

Jess went back inside and began spooning home-cured olives with fennel seeds, garlic and chillies into *maiolica* dishes. All the while thinking of Charlie. She wondered if he still remembered their first kiss. It had been under the light of a lamppost on the corner near her student flat. Big drops of rain were falling, caught in the lamplight, as she looked up into his big brown eyes. *Don't be so soppy* she thought as she got on with her work.

An hour later Jess was looking into those same chocolatey eyes as she took his order. He didn't recognize her immediately, but when he did, he seemed amazed, almost ecstatic. He jumped up from the table and hugged her while his friends looked on bemused.

After he'd eaten, Charlie insisted on leaving his friends at the table and helping her in the kitchen before walking her home. As they worked, they chatted about old times. Conversation flowed easily between them. They had nearly twelve years of catching up to do. Somehow, she realized, she had imagined that he was single. He wasn't wearing a ring, but he told her he was living with an older woman. He seemed a bit embarrassed to tell her that she had been one of his tutors in London. Jess wondered if she had been the reason why they had drifted apart.

Charlie told her that he'd been in his early twenties when he'd fallen in love with Melinda. Jess was surprised to feel a pang of jealousy that he could love someone else. She told herself she was being silly. After all, she had loved Maurizio with all her heart. Charlie continued to talk about this woman, Melinda. She had been in her late forties. He said he'd found her so different. She was very intellectual and sophisticated. She had travelled to so many places teaching English and researching.

Charlie was suddenly quiet. Then he told her that over the years their relationship had changed. At first, she was the one who knew all about food and wine. Her clothes had designer labels that he'd never heard of. She took him to art galleries and fashion shows and top restaurants. At university she was his tutor and outside of campus she tutored him in other ways. She was incredibly at ease with her body and her sexuality and very experienced. Charlie had fallen for her and for the style of life she wanted to share with him. It was all so different from student accommodation, tinned beans and warm beer. Then, slowly, he had gained in confidence and she had got older.

They had set off through the dark lanes under the light of the moon. It was a beautiful walk in the evening. When they got back to Jess's house, they were still talking, so she invited him in for coffee which they drank sitting in comfortable chairs in the kitchen, the dogs and the cat sleeping nearby. Charlie said he felt awful about the whole thing but the truth was that Melinda was nearly sixty and he was still a young man. His academic career was just taking off as she was thinking about retirement. He wanted to get married and have children and, while he still cared about her, they had been living separate lives for years. He had just never got around to leaving her.

Jess wasn't sure what to think. The situation he described made her feel sad. She knew what it was like to want to start a family. Charlie had asked her about what she had been up to but she didn't feel ready to talk about her past. *Maybe another time* she thought. Charlie took the hint and, standing up, he said, 'you must be tired.' She showed him to the door and, as he brushed past her, the old flame reignited and they found themselves kissing passionately. Jess pulled away. Charlie looked confused. They wished each other goodnight and she closed the door behind him. A moment later he was back, asking to see her the next day. She said *yes*.

The following evening, after dinner with his friends, Charlie walked Jess home again. This time, when they arrived at the little house, he pulled her into him and kissed her. The old passion was still there. Jess was breathless with the feel of him. The taste of him. As the dogs ran around outside, she led him into the guest bedroom on the ground floor. The guest room that had never had guests. They undressed each other slowly. Tentatively at first. Then more passionately. They made love like they never had before.

When his friends left for the next leg of their tour, Charlie stayed behind and the two of them spent the next three weeks together. Jess hadn't felt so happy in a long time. They made each other no promises. Told each other no lies. And yet. And yet, Jess expected him to stay. Expected him to leave his old life and move there. Expected to find the happiness that she had lost as though it were her right.

One evening as they lay in each other's arms listening to the chirping of the crickets through the open window, Charlie told her that he was leaving the next day. He had to go back to

Melinda. He would join the boys in France and return as though nothing had happened. *Nothing? Am I nothing? Has this meant nothing to you?* Jess had raged at him, hurt and in shock.

But Jess wasn't willing to accept pain into her life again. She told him to leave and went straight back to her old life. If she were *nothing* to him, then he would be *nothing* to her. She even surprised herself, and Rosa, by accepting to go on a date with the drummer in a group that was playing at the hotel one evening.

It might have started as an act of revenge. Of defiance directed at Charlie. But Jess found herself falling for Ruiz. He was strong and dependable and funny. He was attentive and kind and romantic. When she could, she would go to his concerts and felt excited at being *the drummer's girlfriend*. Ruiz loved to cook for her and she adored a man who cooked. It all seemed so perfect. Except, perhaps, for one thing. Their love making was comfortable and safe. She felt safe for the first time in years. But it was not passionate. It was not amazing. *Perhaps she was asking for too much.*

Then, the messages from Charlie had started to arrive and she had quickly fallen into the habit of talking to him every day. Though he told her he loved her and texted several times a day, whenever she asked about Melinda, he would clam up. After a few weeks, Jess began to get bored of their repetitive conversations about his work or what the weather was like in England. She felt awful when he was unable to talk to her. 'For obvious reasons', he would say. She felt as though she was cheating on Ruiz. So, she told him to stop calling.

One Monday night in late September, Ruiz had prepared them paella and was just opening the wine as something fell out of his pocket. Jess bent down automatically to pick it up and was surprised to see it was a ring box. Ruiz got down on one knee and took the box off her, opening it up to reveal a beautiful emerald engagement ring. Before he could say anything, her phone rang.

When Jess answered it, the voice on the other end of the telephone told her she might want to sit down. Jess perched on the edge of the sofa and waited for the police to give her the bad news. Then the doorbell rang. Ruiz shrugged and went to open the door for her. The voice on the end of the phone told her that her husband, Maurizio, had been found. He was alive and well but had been suffering from amnesia after an accident on his scooter. He had been living a different life in Rome, but suddenly his memory had returned and he wanted to see her. Just then, Ruiz came back into the room. 'There's some guy in Lycra at the door with a great big sign that says *I've left Melinda. Will you marry me?*' he said.

Little Jay

My mother doesn't like any of her children, but she keeps on having them. Anabella, the latest addition to the family, is the seventh. A red-faced, ugly baby. Plump and scrunched and whinging. I can see my mother is already becoming disenchanted with her.

I wonder why she keeps on having more. My sister says it's because she's an eternal optimist and is hoping to get one that she likes. My brother says it's Papa's fault. How can that be true? Papa is a good man. A kind and happy man. He, unlike my mother, loves us all. Okay, he doesn't love us in equal measure but I'm sure he does his best. His favourite is Jay-Jay. He calls her his Little Jay.

In the afternoons when we all get back from school, Papa takes Jay-Jay walking through the olive groves. I watch them from Harry's bedroom window at the very top of the house (the eldest boy deserves a room of his own). They go up the path towards the chicken coops that Billy Redson keeps. Dirty, smelly things they are. Good eggs though, with slippery yellow yolks. Hand in hand they go. Jay-Jay in her white *broderie anglaise* dress and summer sandals. She likes to wear Mamma's straw hat even though it's too big for her.

When they reach the top of the hill, Papa puts a blanket down on the dry grass and Jay-Jay lies down obediently like a good girl. Like a trusting puppy. Mamma's hat is discarded now. And Papa lays beside her and tickles her under the chin with a freshly picked daisy. 'To see if you like butter' he says. And Jay-Jay laughs and tells him that you don't do it with daisies. You have to do it with buttercups. They laugh so loud I swear I can hear them from the open window.

Then Mamma calls that dinner is ready and I smell the fresh-baked cobs and beef stew with dumplings. *Padded-out* Mamma says. All our food is padded out with potatoes and rice and pasta and dumplings. Not much meat. 'Got to make it go further. Lots of stodge to get some fat on our bones. Joey has the loudest voice. He opens the back door and shouts that dinner is ready. But Papa never answers when he's having fun with his Little Jay.

Love me not

Those weekends were so deliciously exciting. Of course, she felt guilty about having Richard in the house while Gerald was away on business. But his suggestion of going to a hotel had seemed, well, sordid. And, being a practical woman, it was also cheaper this way and more discreet. She could not share her marital bed with another man so they had sex in the Guest Room and showered in the Guest Bathroom and ate their meals in the conservatory.

She loved cooking for Richard. Gerald was such a boring old fart with his meat and two veg and his apple crumble. With Richard, she could experiment, in the kitchen *and* in the bedroom. She had thought her naughty underwear days were long gone but here she was approaching fifty and discovering things she had never even dreamed of. This weekend she would have creamy lemon chicken piccata and a half-Italian lover who was nearly half her age.

Although he repeated often that he didn't love her and she had no reason not to believe what he said, when Richard looked into her eyes as they made love, he looked exactly like a man in love as he whispered, '*Quanto sei bella*' (how beautiful you are). When she told him that she loved him he would ask if she felt loved in return and she would answer, truthfully, '*yes*'. And he would nod and smile, satisfied. He said he wanted her to feel loved but he didn't love her. He once told her that if he could have loved anyone, he would have loved her. So, at the time, she thought of him as being unable to love. Though, she couldn't help but ask herself why he wanted her to feel loved if he did not love her. *Was it all a cruel game?*

While Helen and Richard were holed up in the guest bedroom playing mind games, Gerald was enjoying his freedom. He had a suite booked at the Acqua Sana spa for himself and his gorgeous secretary, Olga. A few more weekends away and he would be able to stop paying Richard for his services. Once he could be sure of Olga's feelings for him, he would return home early one weekend and catch his wife and her lover in flagrante. No way was that miserable cow getting her hands on his savings. All she'd ever given him was indigestion with her repetitive meat and two veg and stodgy puddings followed by boring sex with the lights out.

After Richard left Helen's house, he would drive back to his seaside apartment and tell his wife all about his horrendous weekend humping a boring housewife for money and Olga would tell him how she'd had to grit her teeth and look at the ceiling as she felt the dead weight of her boss upon her.

Then they would laugh out loud and Richard would open a bottle of champagne and they would make a toast to their future and all the money they were going to make out of the stupidest couple in the world...

Dinner for Two

I had been hoping for a little less light in the restaurant. Something more intimate for my first date in Italy. Not total darkness, of course. Although I seem to remember reading somewhere about a restaurant where people eat naked in the dark with complete strangers.

I was smiling to myself as I tried to imagine eating pasta in the dark whilst covering my *family jewels*, when the door opened and in walked my date. The dark yellow dress she was wearing showed off her slim figure and a great late summer tan. Long dark hair fell in curls over her shoulders. *Yes. Yes. Thank you, Aunt Teresa. You did a great job!*

My mother's aunt is in her eighties. I've been staying with her for three months as I'm doing a course at the University of Turin. When she had commented on the fact that I never go out and offered to set me up with someone, I'm not sure what I had expected, but it was not the woman who was now telling me her name. I missed it of course. I stuck out my hand in greeting and managed to poke her in the ribs as she reached in to kiss my cheek. I then lunged forward aiming for her cheek and somehow kissed her ear.

Luckily, the waiter arrived to show us to our table. Not so luckily, it was in the very centre of the crowded restaurant. Had I been rude enough to stick my elbows out whilst eating, I would have hit the man on my left and, probably, also the woman to my right. I smiled and took the menu that was being offered me, knocking over a large vase of flowers in the middle of the table. Luckily, my date had quick reflexes and managed to catch them.

Embarrassed and feeling rather warm, I stood up to take my jacket off and banged my head on the silver lampshade which hung so low that it skimmed the top of the flowers, blocking my view of *the lady in yellow* as I had now come to think of her. I wondered how I could ask her name again without seeming like an idiot. I held out my hand and said, 'should we start again? I'm Paul, nice to meet you'. She smiled and shook my hand and said, 'Serena. Likewise.'

I sat down and tried desperately to think of something to say. My eyes settled on the aforementioned flowers. Like most men, I know absolutely nothing about flowers. *Should I say that? Is it sexist?* I said it anyway. I then commented on the fact that all I knew was that they weren't roses. And that was my horticultural knowledge well and truly exhausted. Serena smiled politely.

I tried to think of another topic of conversation. My mother would describe me as a *slow burner*. I'm not sure what she means by that. I'm not sure why I've never asked her. I would describe myself as painfully shy and a bit of a geek. I scanned the wine list and the menu looking for inspiration.

We settled on the zucchini risotto and a bottle of white wine. I know nothing about wine but the waiter nodded as though it were a suitable choice. I asked him to remove the flowers too. At least now I could see Serena better and I liked what I saw. She smiled and said, 'ah, you like my dress.' It wasn't really the dress that I was interested in and, as if she had read my mind, Serena continued, 'you will like what is underneath it more'.

I must have turned the colour of the red wine they were drinking on the next table, just as the waiter arrived with the risotto. I thought of something to say about courgettes, but then decided that perhaps they were too phallic to be a polite topic of conversation so we ate in relative silence. Relative, that is, only to our table as the rest of the restaurant was buzzing with conversation.

'Guess!' Serena said suddenly. And thinking that she must be talking about the colour of her underwear, I blushed again and went through all the colours I could think of, from black, white and beige to turquoise, pink and orange. Serena laughed. She had a deep laugh and such a pretty mouth. Her lipstick was applied perfectly and did not seem to come off when she licked her lips, something that she seemed to be doing a lot of.

The waiter arrived to take our plates away and brought us a candle to replace the flowers he had removed earlier. *Great. Something else to knock over. Perhaps I could even set the place on fire before dessert.* Serena by candlelight and after half a bottle of wine was starting to look lovelier than ever. I wondered whether she would invite me back to her place. I couldn't really take her back to Aunt Teresa's house.

'So, you have not guessed. You must come to my home and I will show you.' Serena seemed to be reading my mind again. Her English was very good and I told her so. She surprised me by telling me that she had had a lot of English boyfriends. I wondered how many *a lot* was and started to worry about how I would compare. Obviously, I thought it would be unfavourably. Serena seemed to be enjoying the evening.

To finish the meal, we ordered chocolate profiteroles. We chatted some more about our hobbies, the weather. Banal things. I had hoped that some sparkling wit might suddenly spring from nowhere to my aid, but it was not to be. Serena did not seem to be put off. She was licking chocolate off her fork with a surprisingly long tongue.

Now there was the dilemma of who should pay for the meal. *Was it offensive if I offered? Was it rude if I didn't? Was it childish to go halves?* The waiter resolved the problem by bringing the bill to me. Serena sat quietly waiting for me to pay.

We said goodnight to the restaurant staff and walked into the cool evening air. After a very short walk, we arrived at Serena's building. Her apartment was on the top floor. With no lift. I arrived huffing and puffing and red in the face. Serena walked up all five floors in high heels without even getting out of breath.

Her apartment had an amazing view over the city and a small balcony to sit outside. It had plain white walls and a few pink cushions but was much more minimalist than I was expecting. I waited for Serena to offer me coffee but she didn't. Instead, she told me again that I had not guessed. I tried, frantically, to think of more colours. 'Mauve?' I tried. She laughed deeply and repeated the word several times as though she had never heard it before. I laughed too as though the word *mauve* was suddenly the funniest word in the world.

Then she unzipped her dress and let it fall to the floor. She was not wearing *any* underwear at all but that was not the thing she thought I would like. I looked at it and looked at her and was, again, lost for words. 'Do you like him?' she said eventually. And I thought about it a moment before I said, 'yes. Yes, I rather think I do!'

Eleven

We lay on our backs in the long summer grass with our arms folded behind our heads looking at the vastness of the sky and the tumbling fluffy clouds. Somehow, we thought that the answers to everything were up there in the blueness of our futures.

A green metallic beetle crawled up a blade of grass, clinging on to its road to whatever destiny had in store for it. It was beautiful. At the top of the blade, it toppled off and landed in the pile of bluebells that we'd picked.

Stephen was the dinner monitor at junior school. He always gave me extra pudding and I let him copy off me in tests. He wasn't the brightest boy in the class but he was the best looking and my first 'love'.

Stephen had a mop of dark curly hair and big blue eyes. He was always kind, but naughty.

The day the girls had their talk about sex education, we were shown a video, and given a booklet to explain things more fully. Stephen had been one of the group of boys peering through the glass door. Mrs Harnet had shooed them away and pulled the curtain further across the glass.

The booklet was bright pink and was called *All about my Vagina*. Stephen and I had our first argument that day. He was adamant that he knew what the book was called and I insisted that he didn't. In the end, to prove his case, he blurted out, 'It's called *All about my Regina!*'

I didn't understand why he got so mad at me for laughing. I did try to explain to him what Regina meant but he insisted he was right and that was that. I never did like confrontation. Even as a child.

For a while he gave me very small portions of pudding and slopped my custard so that it splashed me on the arms or, sometimes, on my dress. I didn't retaliate and gradually things returned to normal.

I can't remember whose idea it was to go to Barrow Park that afternoon or why we had decided to pick bluebells. I took them home to my mother and she shouted at me because it wasn't allowed. I felt so hurt that she hadn't appreciated the gesture.

I thought we were having a lovely time but suddenly Stephen gave me all his bluebells and said he had to go. I thought he must have to be back for tea. 'Don't tell anyone!' he said. And I didn't.

Not long after that, he wore a green t-shirt to school one day and I went off him. How fickle love is when you are eleven. That summer we left school and went our separate ways. Stephen was sent away to boarding school and I moved to Cambridge and started at an all-girls' school. Those were the worst days of my life.

Nine or ten years later, I was in town with some friends and spotted Stephen in the Dog and Trumpet. He still had his mop of dark hair and his silly grin. He came over to our table and, rather drunkenly, insisted that he knew me. I remember beaming from ear to ear and feeling touched that he remembered me. Then he said, 'I know you. You're, you're, you're Denise Fitton'.

Denise Fitton was the girl who had sat next to me for four years. I can still remember the disappointment.

The Word

We sat underneath great awnings in the field on Harper Way, waiting for the miracle to happen. An old woman in a purple dress, clutching a rooster, was dancing barefoot on the parched grass. All the cats this side of the river were howling and a hollering as though they were being skinned alive. Then, the sky came down. It was so dark and low that it nearly touched the men's hats and grabbed them clean away.

Then, the older boys arrived with wheelbarrows and trolleys, piled high with trays of fish pie and pickles. There was enough to feed the whole town. We ate and we sang, and we danced ourselves into a frenzy. Pastor Joe shouted Hallelujah and Praise Be! We all joined in with our Hallelujahs and our Praise the Lords.

As the clock on the church struck five, the girls from the choir stood up and sang and even the cats stopped wailing and listened to those sweet-as-honey melodies.

The heavens turned purple and crimson before the sun broke through like brimstone. A murmuring began until the noise filled the whole field. Louder than summer crickets it was.

As we shielded our eyes and held our breath, the sky began to smoke and bubble. Silence spread through the crowds like wildfire. Then, just as we were thinking that our skin would burn and split, *He* appeared before us. So bright that we dare not give him more than a stolen glance before we returned our eyes to the ground in front of us.

Hope was bursting out of that hush like dammed waterfalls when the rainy season comes. And so began his word…

Slowly

The pain was bad. Worse than ever this morning. She wanted to go into the next town, to the supermarket she knew, but she couldn't make it. So, she parked the car and went to a different place. Some days – days like today - the pain medication didn't kick in. They needed food. She had no choice. She walked up and down the unfamiliar aisles, not finding what she wanted. Sometimes finding something similar. She was tired. She was confused.

Suddenly she found herself looking at toothpaste. There were twelve tubes at home because every time she went to the supermarket, she bought another. She remembered that there was no shampoo, *or was it conditioner*? She couldn't remember. The only thing worse than the pain and the confusion was the memory loss. It was embarrassing. She wondered how quickly it would progress.

She was still a young woman. *Her whole life ahead of her.* She'd always found it irritating when people said that. *Everyone* had their whole lives ahead of them. Some of those lives were long and happy. Some, like hers, were short and painful.

Now, every item that she picked up was sending shooting pains through her arms. She could only choose products from one level. The pain in her back stopped her from bending. Her shopping bag was already too heavy for her to hold. It was always a balancing act. More shopping meant more days before she'd have to go again. But more shopping also meant heavier bags and more pain. She carried on. Not just for the family but for herself. She carried on trying to seem normal.

Feeling queasy and faint, she joined the queue to pay. The woman in front of her was on her phone. Rebecca willed her to stop talking and put her shopping on the conveyor belt. A long queue was forming behind her now. At last, it was her turn. She placed the items carefully. As quickly as she could. The woman in front of her was still talking on her phone. She had not put her shopping away yet.

Rebecca's items were building up and she couldn't get them into the plastic bags quickly enough. The bags wouldn't open. Some of them ripped. The cashier sighed and tutted. Rebecca tried to put her things away. The pain was almost unbearable. She did her best. Her husband always told her she could only do her best.

Suddenly, the cashier was demanding to be paid. Telling her that she was slow. Telling her that she was holding up the queue. The women behind her began nodding and agreeing. Rebecca tried to put her shopping away and get her money out. Her fingers fumbled with the clasp on her purse. She couldn't seem to get her card out or her money.

The cashier was telling the woman behind her how slow she was. Then she started calling her names. They were all laughing by now. Like a pack of wild animals surrounding their prey. She imagined them killing her and eating her.

She tried to say she was sorry but that only made things worse. The whole queue was joining in now. Sneering and insulting her. They had mistaken her apologies for some kind of retaliation. Rebecca wasn't sure what was happening.

The woman in front of her finally finished her phone call and moved away. She tried again to explain herself but they laughed and accused her of wanting the last word. Eventually, she paid, took her heavy bags and limped back to the car; their taunts still ringing in her ears.

She sat with her head on the steering wheel and cried hot tears. She felt childish for thinking that life was so unfair. Then, she took a deep breath and drove home.

Later, she made the mistake of telling her husband when he came home. He was a man convinced that people got what they deserved. (She wondered what she had done to deserve *this*.) He was sure that *those evil bitches would burn in hell*. She was sure they wouldn't. She wished them well. She knew that life was unfair and she accepted it.

The following day, she returned to the same shop. She checked that it was the same cashier. When it was her turn, she put her shopping on the conveyor belt one item at a time as slowly as she could. Then she put her items into bags. Again, as slowly as she could.

The day after, she phoned her friend Angela and they went shopping together. When it was their turn, they put their items on the conveyor belt as slowly as they could. The following day, Maria decided to go with them.

A month later, there were seven of them. All moving as slowly as they could. The cashier didn't know what to do. There was no law against shopping slowly.

The Cat's Tongue

Does only one item constitute a Bucket List? Emily wasn't entirely sure. She felt that she should have a long list of things that she wanted to do before she shuffled off this earth, yet the only desire in life that she hadn't managed to achieve, was to publish a book on witchcraft.

She had grown up near the Pendle hills and had developed an unhealthy, so her father said, fascination for spells and witchcraft when she'd come across *Simple Spells for Beginners* (written in 1974 by Sarah Stringer) in a second-hand bookshop in Porlten-le-Dale. Perhaps, in the future, she would add other things to her Bucket List.

Emily hadn't had what could be considered a particularly easy life. Her father was an angry man who believed that children should be seen and not heard. When the mood took him, usually after some quarrel with one of his colleagues, he would lock her in the cellar. It was dark and damp but Emily was not afraid. She accepted it.

When she was a little older, he would torment her by making her stand on the stairs with a cushion. If she got tired and sat down (he would fling open the door and try to catch her by surprise), he would take his belt to her. Across the buttocks where nobody could see. He did not want anyone *noseying* in his business.

The abuse she suffered regularly, until she ran away to get married, was not always physical. Emily's father seemed to glean great satisfaction from trying to frighten her. He threatened her regularly with boarding school or being thrown out. Emily thought she would have enjoyed boarding school immensely.

One of her father's favourite rants was that he would *make her pay*. She was able to shut out the abuse, but the thought that he was doing this to make her pay for something, niggled in her mind. She was an intelligent, curious child. When Emily didn't answer back, but stood in silence, her father would get angrier than ever. *What's the matter? Cat got your tongue?* He would always say and then snigger.

Before her father had stopped talking, he used to tell her to *get back to her own father*. Emily began to wonder who *her own father* was and whether she should start looking for him and why she had been living with this awful man since her mother's disappearance if he were not her father.

Then, she had met Rick and they'd moved in together. They'd opened a little café in Church Brow. It wasn't as near the sea as they would have liked, but business had flourished. In the eighties, they'd bought bigger premises and added a take-away service. The children had come along. First

Matilda, then Thomas and finally, Rose. Emily had no spare time to study spells and her project was put on hold, as tends to happen so often in life.

Time passed quickly. Business was not booming, more ticking along nicely. The children were nearly grown-ups and had their own lives. She and Rick had been able to take on a couple of young girls from the village. Life was good. Emily thought again about her book on witchcraft. She was still looking for one particular spell to reverse a hex.

One Thursday morning, she received a phone call. Rick had been hit on the head by a roof tile on St. Oswald Street. He'd been dead before the ambulance had arrived, twenty-three minutes later. She was now a widow.

Emily had loved Rick, but she accepted things, the way she always had. She sold the house and the café and bought herself a little cottage on the coast with steps leading down to a lovely sandy bay. It wasn't private but very few people seemed to use it and she could see the sea from the kitchen window and from the front bedroom. She was happy enough.

Now she would have the time to look for the spell she needed and to get her witchcraft book finished and published. Somehow, she always seemed to be too busy. First, she freshened up the cottage with a lick of paint. Then, she started on the garden, buying plants and bulbs from a lovely local nursery. Unpacking had seemed to take forever. She was tired.

A short walk down the road from the cottage was The Jolly Roger. Emily was not much of a drinker but she had started to go for lunch on Tuesdays as a treat. On cooler days she would have steak pie and chips and when the weather got warmer, she would have steak pie and salad.

One day she had seen an advert, *Kittens! Free to a good home.* Emily asked herself if she could offer a good home to a kitten and decided that she could, so she telephoned the number. The lady who answered, Mrs. Thornton, seemed very nice. They agreed that she would take the only remaining girl, a little black cat with one white paw.

After her usual Tuesday lunch, Emily drove towards town and out through the country lanes to Pear Tree Cottage where she shared a nice cup of tea, and a lovely chat about the weather, with Mrs. Thornton. She put Alice Nutter on a blanket in a box on the back seat. She was looking forward to the company. She'd never had a pet.

Alice Nutter seemed to settle in quickly. She was a happy little soul. Emily went back to researching her book at the local library. She planned on publishing it in early Autumn, but first she needed to find the elusive spell. She needed a spell to reverse the curse that she had put on her father when she'd walked out at just sixteen. Emily wanted him to speak again so that she could ask him who her real father was.

Acknowledgements

Thank you to Riccardo Deri for believing in me and for being there when my lack of technological expertise would have driven a lesser man to distraction. My heart is broken that you left me too soon.

Thank you to my son, Matteo Federico Saveri, who has filled my heart with love and found time in his busy schedule, to answer Mami's many questions on how to do this. Thank you for reading my stories and telling me you love them.

Thanks again to Martine Greslon-Collins for your friendship, your kindness, your praise and encouragement; and, not least, for providing me with this wonderful peaceful place in which to write. I shall miss you immensely when I leave *Freddie old girl*. I must remember not to wear mascara that day.

A wider thank you goes to those many teachers, tutors and lecturers who instilled in me a passion for words and showed me patience.

Thanks also to others who have read my work and told me to write more, and to my biggest fan and fellow Northerner, Anita Summers-Manuzi, a very persistent woman. I dare not list other names, as I would hate to leave anyone out.

*

Printed by Amazon Italia Logistica S.r.l.
Torrazza Piemonte (TO), Italy

41343627R00098